Personal Retributions

Andrew French

This is a work of fiction. All characters, names, places and incidents are either the product of the author's imagination or fictionalised, and any resemblance to actual people, locations or events is coincidental.

Copyright © 2013 Andrew French

All rights reserved.

ISBN-10:1481959913
ISBN-13:978-1481959919

DEDICATION

For all my family and friends for their continued love and support.

CHAPTER ONE

It was hot in Paris, hotter than was usual for August. The Parisian mass exodus had begun to the over-packed beaches of the Cote d'Azur. The muggy streets, stripped of their usual metropolitan stress levels, were now besieged by tourists from all around the world. In the melee of the early afternoon Paris traffic, a dark red Volvo estate gradually progressed east down the Champs-Elysée. Inside the car, amid the constant sound of impatient car horns, the two men and one woman sat in silence as they negotiated the free-for-all of the city's chaotic road network.

Their journey had been a long one and they looked weary with the heat and pale with fatigue. The previous day, on Monday 11[th,] the battered ten year old Volvo had left Belfast in darkness shortly before dawn. Francis O'Sullivan, a short man in his early fifties, had embraced the three in turn and wished them luck. The young woman smiled briefly and nodded, ignoring her father's concerned expression. At thirty, Roisin was the eldest of his three children and his only daughter. His two sons, Martin and Robert, got into the car assuring him that they would be back by the end of the week.

"Are you sure you won't change your mind and come back with your brothers?" O'Sullivan asked as the girl opened the rear door. "We don't see or hear from you in almost two years then you turn up here out of the blue a fortnight ago only to disappear again."

"I'm sorry daddy but there are things I have to do; important things."

"With this mysterious boyfriend of yours, I suppose."

"You haven't met him. He's got a fire and a passion that takes my breath away."

"So what is this thing that you have to do? What could be more important than being here with your family where you belong? Why did you really come back?"

"You'll see." Roisin said with a cold, confident voice. "Soon the whole world will see." She smiled again, that sweet innocent lovely smile that belied her true icy character. "First I've got this wee present to deliver." She patted the roof of the car with her palm and got in. Tapping her brother on the shoulder, she told him to get going. The Volvo pulled away and headed out of the notorious Twinbrook Estate for the ferry terminal. As O'Sullivan watched the car disappear into the darkness, passing the innocuous looking Commer van parked fifty yards down the street, the two surveillance men inside radioed that the target was on the move.

The secret army intelligence unit colloquially known as The Det had been watching the terraced house on Glasvey Drive round the clock for the last two weeks. Francis O'Sullivan and his boys were known to be active members of the IRA. Francis had been recruited in 1970 when his wife, Theresa, was shot accidentally by the British Army during a shoot-out with the IRA on the Falls Road. Seeking an outlet for his rage against those he considered murdered his wife, the Provisional IRA welcomed him. Exploiting his grief and anger, they gave him many opportunities to exact his revenge during the following years.

The O'Sullivans' activities were routinely monitored by the intelligence services but it was when Roisin O'Sullivan returned home that The Det's interest peaked. Graduating in 1979 from

Belfast University, she gained a first reading chemistry. Indoctrinated by her father as a child, she had an all consuming hatred for the British and was thought to be responsible for making some of the most devastating car bombs of the early 1980's. In 1984, when a bomb-making factory in Newry was raided by the special forces, Roisin narrowly avoided capture and fled the country, deciding to travel abroad for a while.

It was a little after six and the sun was rising on the ferry terminal when the Volvo arrived. As they queued to board the car ferry the O'Sullivans were unaware of the beige Ford Sierra that had discreetly followed them from the Twinbrook Estate. The Sierra slowed as the four man Det team watched the Volvo prepare to board the ship then joined the queue, five cars behind.

Having docked at Liverpool mid afternoon, the Det team followed the Volvo down to Dover where the O'Sullivans spent the night in a small bed and breakfast. This gave Mitchell, the team commander, an opportunity to examine the car. It didn't take him long to discover the fifty pounds of concealed plastic explosive wired to a remote control detonator which was packed into the spare wheel compartment in the boot floor.

The following morning at seven o'clock, Robert O'Sullivan was the first to emerge. He cautiously looked around before getting into the car. Martin and Roisin soon followed and minutes later they melted into the Dover rush hour traffic. As they followed, several cars behind, Mitchell had a growing sense of unease as the Volvo filtered into the lane for the Dover car ferry thirty minutes later. His fears were realised as they headed straight for the waiting car ferry bound for Calais. The Sierra pulled up in the car park close by.

Mitchell shouted for quiet amid a torrent of profanity as they realised they were going to lose their target. Radioing Det HQ at RAF Aldergrove, he waited anxiously having requested instructions.

"We can't lose them, Mitch," Sheridan said from the back seat, leaning forward to Mitchell's ear. "You know what's in that car." Mitchell didn't reply. He stared intently at the target vehicle, gripping the radio handset. Seconds later it crackled to life and they heard the familiar voice of their commanding officer telling them to stand by.

At Aldergrove, Colonel Charles Mabbitt stood in the hushed communications room with his second in command, Major Dickinson. Mabbitt slowly rubbed his eyebrow as he considered his response.

"You're not seriously considering allowing them to proceed, are you?" Dickinson said warily. "You can't do that. Colonel, I think you'd be making a terrible mistake." Mabbitt's eyes flashed a withering glance.

"Thank you, Nigel but unless I'm very much mistaken this unit has yet to become a democracy. I'm sure that when that glorious day arrives a sweetly scented missive will wing its way from our lords and masters. Until then, I believe it is my will that prevails." Mabbitt opened the microphone. "This is Mabbitt. You are authorised to maintain surveillance on the vehicle and determine its target. You are to be robust in the prevention of the detonation of that device. Clear?" There was a palpable sense of relief in the car as Mitchell confirmed the order.

"You know that we don't have any jurisdiction once we get off that ferry, don't you?" Franklyn warned Mitchell earnestly from the back.

"Better not get caught then, had we?" he replied sharply, nodding to Connor behind the wheel. "Let's go."

It was two-thirty by the time the O'Sullivans entered Paris. Still unaware that they were being followed, Roisin had finally insisted on silence, tired and irritated by her brothers' constant bickering and petty squabbling. As hard as the two men were, they knew that when their sister gave an order they did as they were told. Roisin not only had the brains of the family, she also had more natural killer instinct than both of the boys combined. She had no compunctions concerning what they were about to do or the large number of innocent people who were going to be killed or injured.

The Volvo turned into the *Rue du Faubourg St Honoré*, slowing as they approached number Thirty-Five. Martin O'Sullivan parked twenty yards from the towering, dark brown, ornately carved double doors of the British Embassy.

"This is it," Mitchell said as Connor pulled the Sierra over a safe distance away. He ordered Sheridan to break out the weapons and he did so excitedly. As Sheridan opened the hidden compartment behind the rear central arm rest and began distributing the Browning automatic pistols, Roisin and her brothers were out of the car and walking away from them. Seconds later the Det team had split into two. Sheridan and Franklyn crossed the street and walked parallel to Mitchell and Connor who remained behind the three targets. Both teams blended into the crowds of tourists as they followed unnoticed thirty yards behind. Turning right into the *Rue Royale* and heading towards *La Place de la Concorde* and the *Jardin de Tuileries*, the O'Sullivans walked casually in the bright Parisian sunshine, appearing to be nothing more sinister than another three foreign tourists.

The *Champs Elysees* was filled with a combination of the ultra chic with their huge sunglasses and designer labels and the ordinary sightseer enjoying the French capital's most famous thoroughfare. The people watchers in the countless street cafés sipped their iced *citron presses* as they relaxed at their tables beneath the huge white sun umbrellas that offered much needed shade.

It was one of these pavement cafés the O'Sullivans entered and stood together. Sheridan and Franklyn stopped and watched the three talking quietly as Mitchell and Connor continued walking past the café to a news stand. As they picked up a copy of *Le Figaro* they watched Roisin kiss her brothers on the cheek and leave the café. At the news stand, Mitchell and Connor turned away as she walked past them throwing her handbag onto her shoulder. Moments later Sheridan and Franklyn arrived at the stand.

"You two keep an eye on the brothers Grimm over there. If they look as if they're going to detonate the bomb, take them out then make yourself scarce. Got it?" Mitchell ordered under his breath. Sheridan and Franklyn both nodded. "We're going after Crystal Tipps and see what she's up to. 'RV' back at the car."

While Sheridan and Franklyn took up position at a table that afforded them a clear view of where the O'Sullivan brothers were sitting, Mitchell and Connor were pursuing Roisin. She was walking quickly now as if late for an appointment. As her pace quickened, the two Det men got the distinct feeling Roisin had a very different agenda to that of her brothers. Periodically she would glance over her shoulder but each time didn't seem to notice the two men following her in the crowd.

At the pavement café Robert and Martin O'Sullivan drained the last drops of ice cold beer from the glasses that had been brought to them a minute earlier by a superior looking waiter. Franklyn's mouth was dry in the hot afternoon and he could almost taste the Irishmen's beer as he and Sheridan watched them place the empty glasses on the table with a satisfied sigh. The waiter, still wearing the same superior expression, bobbed under Sheridan and Franklyn's sun umbrella and, with his pad and pencil poised, tilted his head forward. Without speaking, he raised his eyebrows. Sheridan glanced up at the condescending Frenchman momentarily. "Two beers," he said abruptly, returning his gaze to the Irishmen.

As the waiter stalked away they watched Martin produce what they recognised to be a remote control detonator from his jacket pocket and hold it in his lap. The two soldiers were already on their feet and making their way towards the O'Sullivans' table as Martin began to extend the steel telescopic antenna. They knew what they had to do. It had to be quick, surgical, to ensure there would be no chance of civilian casualties. It was over in less than five seconds. Sheridan and Franklyn struck, putting four rounds in rapid succession at close range into their unsuspecting targets. Amid terrified screams from the packed café, Sheridan calmly picked up the detonator and the two men hurried away.

As the shots rang out, Roisin instinctively turned and looked back briefly in the direction of the café. That was when she saw two men some twenty yards behind her that made her feel uneasy. They were the only two that hadn't turned round at the sound of the gunshots. She knew instantly her brothers were dead and that she now was being followed. She bit her lip with anger and walked a little faster.

Close to the entrance of the *Champs Elysees Clemenceau* Metro station, Roisin made eye contact with a large, tanned, muscular man in a blue polo shirt and chinos standing nearby. Removing his sunglasses, his smile quickly disappeared as she shook her head. Taking a Marlboro packet from her bag, she tossed it into a dustbin and rushed into the Metro entrance. He watched as two men began to sprint through the crowded street and follow her into the station then turned his attention back to the dustbin.

It took a few minutes for Mitchell to find Roisin on the crowded platform. She turned and stared at him coldly across the sweaty throng of waiting passengers. Mitchell held her gaze as he and Connor slowly moved through the swell of people. She wasn't frightened. Nor did she try to run from her approaching pursuers. She glared at the two men with nothing but contempt and hatred for them. Suddenly, as the soldiers closed to within ten feet of her, Roisin grabbed a young blonde woman standing in front of her. Gripping her tightly round the neck from behind, Roisin pressed a small knife to the terrified woman's throat. The crowd scattered, fleeing up the platform like frightened sheep, leaving Mitchell and Connor facing Roisin.

"Let her go, Roisin. It doesn't have to end like this," Mitchell said. Roisin's eyes narrowed on hearing an English voice.

"British. I suppose you're SAS?"

"Army Intelligence," Mitchell replied. A wry smile appeared at the corners of Roisin's mouth.

"Are you Colonel Mabbitt's boys?" Now it was Mitchell's turn to look surprised. By its very nature, few knew of his unit's existence let alone the name of its commanding officer. "I suggest you let me go or Harry will get very cross, and trust me, you really don't want that."

Connor went to draw his gun but Mitchell stopped him as half a dozen uniformed police officers burst through the crowd with their weapons drawn. Roisin backed towards the edge of the platform near the tunnel entrance, pulling the young woman with her. Deep in the tunnel the low rumble of the approaching train got louder and louder. Shouting at Mitchell and Connor to get back to the rest of the onlookers, the police took up position surrounding Roisin.

"Tell Mabbitt that Harry sends his regards!" she shouted and, pushing the woman away from her, threw herself in front of the train as it emerged from the tunnel behind her. Mitchell and Connor managed to disappear into the crowd in the chaos and confusion that followed, avoiding having to answer some awkward and potentially very damaging questions.

On the long journey back to Aldergrove, Mitchell's confrontation with Roisin O'Sullivan weighed heavily on his mind. Her total lack of fear and her readiness to die rather than be taken alive nagged at him. There was far more to her visit to Paris than to just detonate a car bomb. There was something in her eyes that had unsettled him; something dark, hidden. She had a secret that she would never, could never, reveal. A secret which she was happily prepared to die to keep.

CHAPTER TWO

The desk calendar clicked over to Thursday 14th August 1986 in Colonel Mabbitt's office at RAF Aldergrove near Belfast. It was midnight and Mitchell had been sitting opposite his commanding officer for almost three hours, recounting the operation in Paris in the minutest detail. With the lack of sleep and the intense concentration of his debrief, Mitchell was feeling weary and was now showing visible signs of fatigue. Even the combined stimulants of nicotine and black coffee were failing to maintain his focus.

"I'm sorry, Colonel" Mitchell said apologetically after he finished going through the sequence of events for the umpteenth time. "That's all there is." Mabbitt sat back in his chair and threw down his pencil onto the pad of scribbled notes. Unlike his operator, Mabbitt showed no sign of tiredness. Since Mitchell had radioed through his conversation with Roisin to him during the journey back to base, Mabbitt had become a driven man. Within seconds of speaking to Mitchell from the communications room he had snatched up the phone and barked an order to Lieutenant Parkes. His tone was uncharacteristically aggressive, urgent.

"Parkes, find out everything there is to know about Roisin O'Sullivan from the minute she was born to when her body hit the Metro tracks in Paris."

Mabbitt sat alone in his office waiting for Mitchell's return and ruminated on the operation that had culminated in Paris. He knew exactly who the 'Harry' was that Roisin had referred to. For two years he had searched tirelessly without success for the American assassin who had murdered his wife at their home. Tenaciously he had used back channels, called in favours, anything that might lead to the whereabouts of Harry Grant. All his efforts, however, had been in vain. He knew that Grant was both cunning and resourceful but it was as if the man had dropped off the face of the earth.

By the time Mitchell and the team arrived back Colonel Mabbitt had read and assimilated every page in the inch thick folder that Lieutenant Parkes had prepared on Roisin O'Sullivan. Despite his long journey, Mitchell was told to report to Mabbitt's office without delay. Three hours later The Det Sergeant's debrief continued relentlessly.

"Tell me again what Roisin did when the shots were fired in the pavement café," Mabbitt said as he scanned the pages. Mitchell blew out his cheeks at the thought of going through it yet again.

"Sir, I've..." Mitchell began but Mabbitt's eyes flashed from the file and stared coldly at him.

"Again!" Mabbitt snapped, then his voice softened "If you would be so kind, Nicholas." Mitchell straightened in his chair. Only his mother ever called him Nicholas and only then when he was in trouble.

"Connor and I were following the girl. We were about five hundred yards from the café when the boys took out the brothers. The girl turned on hearing the gunfire and that's when she spotted us and made for the Metro station."

"Are you certain she wasn't aware of your presence before then?"

"Absolutely. No question."

"So why did she leave her brothers at the café and take off on her own? Mabbitt queried. Mitchell didn't have an answer for him. Mabbitt stared at his man thoughtfully then asked him to continue.

"We followed her down. When she saw us she took a girl hostage and..."

"I want you to think very carefully, Mitchell. This is very important," Mabbitt interrupted abruptly. "Did she, at any time from leaving the café to just before she took the girl hostage, appear to you as if she was about to meet somebody? A man; this man?" Mabbitt produced a photograph and tapped it with his finger. Mitchell looked at the picture carefully and shook his head.

"No, Sir, I didn't see anyone like that."

"Think, Nicholas. Are you certain she didn't meet this man? They may not even have spoken?"

"I'm certain, Colonel. She didn't go anywhere near that man. To be honest, she didn't have time. Once she'd seen us she headed straight for the Metro. She didn't even slow down when she threw the empty cigarette packet in the bin at the entrance."

"What did you say?" Mabbitt said. You didn't mention that before." Mitchell looked confused.

"I didn't mention what?" Mabbitt didn't reply as he turned over page after page of the file in front of him until he found what he was looking for.

"Roisin's mother was a chain smoker. Just weeks before she was killed she had been diagnosed with lung cancer; the result of a twenty year, fifty-a-day habit. Roisin was very close to her mother as a child and apparently used to plead with her to give up. Following her mother's death she was a zealous anti-smoker. Which then begs the question why, when being pursued by you and facing possible capture, does Miss O'Sullivan find it necessary to throw away a packet of cigarettes she would never smoke?"

"A dead drop."

"Quite so," Mabbitt said, nodding thoughtfully. "I think she was about to meet this man but, when she realised you were following her, she got rid of whatever it was she was going to give him. He must have been close, very close." He picked up the photograph and looked at it.

"Who is he? This Harry she spoke of?"

"Yes," Mabbitt said distantly, still studying the American's face. "Harry Grant. A former US Navy SEAL and a sadistic murderer of the innocent." There was a long silence. Without looking up, Mabbitt told Mitchell to go and get some sleep.

"Is everything alright, Colonel?" Mitchell asked as he stood to leave. "Is there..."

His question was cut short by a curt "Goodnight, Sergeant. That will be all." Mitchell left without further comment. Once alone, Mabbitt took a photograph of Roisin O'Sullivan from the file and placed the two images side by side on the desk. He stared at them intently and murmured under his breath, "What did you have that was so important you were prepared to die to give it to him?"

Charles Mabbitt lay in bed and watched the first rays of sunlight penetrate the gap in the curtains in his quarters. His grey eyes had lost their usual sparkle having spent the last four hours staring into the darkness deep in thought. He looked across at the large, white, round face of the brass alarm clock that stood next to the telephone on the bedside cabinet; 5.00am. If he was going to make his meeting with the Joint Intelligence Committee at the Cabinet Office in Whitehall at nine, he would need to move smartly.

He mused over the short and less than sweet telephone call he had received the previous afternoon from Sir Neil Peterson, the Chairman of the JIC. Peterson had dispensed with the few pleasantries he usually observed and proceeded to bellow down the phone, apoplectic with rage. His mood was not made any better when Mabbitt had advised him to calm down or he might rupture something. Peterson came straight to the point, his voice getting higher and higher as he demanded Mabbitt's presence in front of his committee to account for mounting an illegal operation in a foreign country. With a shriek of, "Just be here!" in response to Mabbitt glibly explaining that he would do his very best to see what he could do but Thursdays were usually a bit busy, Peterson had slammed down the phone.

Throwing back the bedclothes, Mabbitt swung his legs over the side and reached for the telephone. "Cancel my helicopter to London and have a car ready for me in one hour. I'll drive myself." What he was about to do was contrary to just about every rule there was but Mabbitt felt he had no alternative. Not if he was going to find Grant. "Tell Mabbitt that Harry sends his regards." Roisin's last words stabbed at his very heart. Wherever he was, Grant was still taunting him and that was unacceptable. Mabbitt had vowed that this man was going to pay for the murder of his wife. He knew all too well that this personal vendetta may cost him everything but if that was how it had to be, then so be it.

Having washed and shaved Colonel Mabbitt pulled on a fawn coloured raincoat and buttoned it over his grey herringbone tweed suit. Taking a Browning automatic pistol from the drawer, he slipped it into one of the coat's deep pockets. Fifteen minutes later he was driving the black Ford Granada out of the front gates. The corporal in the car pool had looked more than a little concerned as he handed Mabbitt the car keys. Such a senior officer leaving the camp alone without protection and at such an early hour was irregular to say the least. He knew better, however, than to question why.

It was just after 7.30am by the time Mabbitt reached the Twinbrook Estate, three miles south west of Belfast. Parking on the outskirts on Twinbrook Road, he walked into the council estate arriving at the O'Sullivan house on Glasvey Drive as the milk was being delivered. As Mabbitt held the gate open for the milkman as he returned to his float, there was a sudden agitated flurry in the Commer van parked across the street. One of the Det surveillance men watching the O'Sullivan house shook the other's arm frantically as he peered through his camera's long lens. "It's the boss!" he exclaimed as the camera started clicking furiously. His dozing partner woke with a start and scrambled to look out of the small window, just in time to see their commanding officer knock on the front door.

"Bloody hell, it is him, it's Mabbitt," he said incredulously.

"What do we do?" the first said, still snapping wildly.

"Well you can stop doing that for a start," he said, snatching the camera from him. "Is he alone?"

"Think so. Shouldn't he have a close protection team with him?" The two men looked at each other for a moment. "What are we going to do?"

"Are you kidding, we call it in and ask for instructions I'm not taking responsibility for this one."

It was a couple of minutes before the door opened and Francis O'Sullivan appeared looking unshaven and dishevelled. He glowered at the tall, elderly man standing before him holding his milk bottle. "What do you want?" he grunted.

"A cup of tea might be rather nice," Mabbitt said brightly, handing him the pint of milk and striding inside. O'Sullivan spun round and, amidst a torrent of foul obscenities, started towards the intruder. Mabbitt calmly pulled the gun from his pocket and levelled it at him. O'Sullivan stopped and stood motionless, breathing hard. "Do sit down," Mabbitt said politely. Still clutching the milk bottle, O'Sullivan slowly did as he was told, hatred in his eyes.

"Who are you?"

"I want to ask you a few questions about your daughter, Roisin."

"Roisin's dead; both my boys too," he replied tersely, the raw pain of his loss still etched on his face.

"Occupational hazard when you're a terrorist," Mabbitt said dryly. "I want to know what Roisin was really doing here. It certainly wasn't to make a car bomb to help out the family."

"I don't know who you are but I don't have to tell you a damn thing and there's nothing you can do about it. So why don't you take your gun and your condescending tone and piss off?" O'Sullivan angrily waved the bottle towards the front door. Mabbitt raised an eyebrow and his face became like stone.

"I've got friends in some very low places. It wouldn't take much to arrange for rumours to start that you are not averse to passing on information to the authorities for certain financial inducements. Admittedly these rumours have no basis in fact but..."

"I'm no tout!" O'Sullivan yelled. "No-one would ever believe that."

"Are you certain of that? You know how it is here. There only need be the merest hint of suspicion of you being an informant and it wouldn't be long before you got a visit in the middle of the night. The best you could then hope for is your kneecaps getting some uncomfortably close attention from a hammer." O'Sullivan could see from the English stranger's unwavering stare that this was no idle threat. "Why was Roisin really here?"

"I don't know; just turned up out of the blue. Said she could only stay a couple of weeks, that there was something really important she had to do, but she wouldn't say what. Something to do with a mysterious new boyfriend, Harry, she'd met while travelling in the far east."

"Did she go anywhere or meet anyone while she was here?" Mabbitt pressed. O'Sullivan glared resentfully. "Well? Did she?"

"She met someone at the airport last Friday," O'Sullivan said grudgingly. "The Washington flight."

"Who?"

"I don't know, she..." O'Sullivan was interrupted by a heavy knock at the door. Mabbitt held his finger to his lips and whispered to be quiet. The knock came again, louder and this time accompanied by an elderly male voice calling O'Sullivan's first name. Mabbitt and O'Sullivan stared silently at each other while the voice announced himself as Father Brendan. Getting no response the ageing catholic priest went away muttering incoherently to himself.

"That was the priest," O'Sullivan muttered, barely controlling his anger. "I've got three funerals to arrange. Or had you forgotten?"

"Better three than three hundred," Mabbitt replied coldly. "I'll let myself out the back. We wouldn't want anyone to get the wrong idea, would we?"

As O'Sullivan sat alone he looked at the photograph of himself with his daughter and two sons that stood on the sideboard in a chipped wooden frame. He knew he couldn't trust the man he had watched leave through the high gate at the end of the rear yard. Taking a large metal biscuit tin from the cupboard in the sideboard, he carried it carefully to the armchair and sat down. There was nothing left to live for now. He had no more fight left in him. It had all been swallowed up by grief and loneliness and the certain knowledge of a cruel and ignominious death, branded as a traitor. He reached inside and took out a Browning automatic pistol, identical to the one that had been pointed at him minutes before. With his hands trembling, O'Sullivan swallowed the last of the Irish whiskey from the bottle he had opened the previous evening. Defiantly, he threw it at the wall and wiped the drips from his grey stubbled chin.

Outside the house a dark blue Ford Transit van pulled up sharply. In response to the surveillance men's request for instructions, Major Dickinson had despatched a four man team to very quietly bring the Colonel back to Aldergrove. As the team commander confirmed with the two in the Commer van that Mabbitt hadn't come out, a single shot rang out from inside the house. With their weapons drawn, the four men sprinted from the van. The door yielded with a shoulder charge and the team disappeared inside.

In the communications room at Aldergrove, Dickinson waited impatiently by the radio for the team commander to report. Two minutes later the radio crackled to life. The voice was subdued, hesitant.

"Have you got the Colonel?" Dickinson asked urgently. There was a long pause.

"No, Sir. The Colonel's gone and..." there was another long pause, "O'Sullivan's dead. A single shot to the head with a Browning nine mill." Dickinson swore under his breath then gathered himself.

"Clear out of there now, and the surveillance van. I don't want you to have any RUC involvement. Not yet. Not until I find out what the bloody hell's going on."

CHAPTER THREE

It was five minutes to twelve when the Lynx helicopter landed at Aldergrove. Major Dickinson stood on the apron of the runway and braced himself for was about to come. As the unit's second-in-command he was accustomed to dealing with difficult and sometimes politically sensitive situations but this was different. He had only met the helicopter's passenger once before when he had told Dickinson, rather condescendingly, that he had done surprisingly well for someone with such a limited education, having attended a mere grammar school. It was with considerable trepidation therefore that he watched Sir Neil Peterson stride across the tarmac, his Gieves and Hawkes suit jacket flapping open in the downdraft of the helicopter's rotors offering a flash of the red silk lining.

There were no pleasantries, nor was there any warmth in the briefest of handshakes as Peterson climbed into the waiting car. There was a long silence in the car as it made its way across the base to the administration building. Dickinson decided against trying to make small-talk as the underlying sense of seething anger from the man next to him, staring straight ahead, was palpable.

The silence came to a sudden and abrupt end once the door was closed in Dickinson's office. "Have you found him yet?" Peterson said, addressing Dickinson like a naughty schoolboy.

"No, Sir. Not yet."

"Well that's just not good enough, Major. Not good enough at all. I want to know what's being done to locate him. What about his car? Doesn't it have some kind of tracking device fitted, hmm?"

Peterson's head tilted back and he stared down his nose at Dickinson with disdain.

"Yes, Sir. It does, but he appears to have... turned it off," Dickinson replied reluctantly.

"Wonderful, Major! That's absolutely wonderful." Peterson finally released him from his withering gaze and stomped around the desk and sat down. "This man he's murdered, O'Sullivan."

"With respect, Sir," Dickinson interjected. "We don't know that it was the Colonel who killed him. My men say the shot could have been self inflicted. The handgun used was lying close to the body." He had been with Colonel Mabbitt since the end of 1980, having replaced the treacherous Captain Noble who was found murdered in an Italian hotel room, and wasn't ready to believe the worst, not yet.

"So why did he run, hmm? What on earth was he doing there alone in the first place, hmm?" Before Dickinson could try to answer what, he hated to admit, were perfectly reasonable questions, the door opened.

"Good afternoon, Nigel," Mabbitt said cheerfully as he breezed into the office. "Neil, my dear chap. What an unexpected surprise how lovely to see you." There was a stunned silence as Mabbitt unbuttoned his overcoat. Peterson became aware that his mouth was open and closed it quickly, rising to his feet.

"That will be all, Major," he said brusquely to Dickinson who, although desperate to remain and hear Mabbitt's explanation, obediently left without speaking. Peterson sat down again and stroked the top of his bald head while he composed himself. "You had orders to report to the JIC this morning. Would you care to explain why you disregarded those orders?"

"Yes, I'm terribly sorry about that, Neil, but I discovered that my hairshirt was in the laundry."

"Don't try and be clever with me," Peterson rebuked down his nose. "You were required to explain to my committee why you mounted an operation in a foreign country without official sanction. An explanation I'm still waiting to hear."

"Well, Neil, it's quite simple really," Mabbitt said slowly as if he were explaining something to a small child. "I didn't ask for official approval because I knew I wouldn't have got it."

"What?" Peterson said angrily, the veins in his temples starting to throb.

"And to be quite frank," Mabbitt continued, enjoying the sight of the JIC Chairman trying desperately to control his anger, "I don't trust the French. They shot and almost killed my best man as he was about to capture a target two years ago. I therefore decided that it would be in everybody's best interests if I just didn't inform them."

"The point is, Charles, you didn't inform anyone!" Peterson shouted, banging his fist on the desk. "Again!" He tried to gather himself. "When are you going to realise that you and your unit are accountable? Which brings me to the reason I find myself here rather than in Whitehall. What were you doing at the O'Sullivan house in Belfast this morning?"

"I was making enquiries," Mabbitt replied brightly.

"You don't make enquiries, Charles. That's what the minions are for."

"I like to keep my hand in."

"Does that extend to murder?" Peterson snapped. The smile slowly disappeared from Mabbitt's face and his eyes narrowed.

"O'Sullivan was found shot dead this morning. I suppose you are going to tell me that you didn't kill him."

"He was alive when I left," Mabbitt said simply.

"Well, we've only got your word for that, haven't we?" I'm sorry, Charles. You leave me no alternative than to suspend you from duty pending a full JIC investigation. You will accompany me back to London and be kept under house arrest until this whole sorry mess is resolved." Peterson tried not to look smug but was relishing every moment of this. He had never liked Mabbitt and the feeling was more than reciprocated. As Mabbitt looked at him impassively, the sparkle in his grey eyes had returned.

Peterson stood and tugged at the front of his waistcoat. "You're in hot water, Mabbitt. Do you hear me, the very hottest water. You've gone too far this time. This will finish you if I've got anything to do with it." He paused triumphantly. "Have you got anything to say for yourself?"

Mabbitt thought earnestly for a moment then replied politely, "With all this hot water about is there any chance of a cup of tea?"

The oak longcase clock in the corner of the drawing room of Mabbitt's house in Biddenden chimed the hour with a single bell. Colonel Mabbitt peered at his wristwatch. "Nine o'clock. Time for a nightcap, I think. It has been rather a hectic day." He rose from his high backed brown leather chair and crossed to a small table. Removing the glass stopper from the crystal whiskey decanter, he paused and turned to the serious looking, dark suited figure sitting on the sofa. "Would you care for one? It might make you feel a little less... morose?" There was no reply, just a slow shake of his large balding head. "Of course, what was I thinking? Not while you're on duty," Mabbitt said as he poured himself a generous malt, gesturing to the Grandfather clock. "That clock is two hundred years old and still keeps perfect time. It was made by Jeremiah Standring, you know." The man stared at him, uninterested in the old man's rambling attempt at small-talk.

Having been flown by helicopter from Aldergrove to Kent, he now found himself under house arrest while he was under investigation for the suspected murder of Francis O'Sullivan. Peterson had been keen not to involve the civilian police preferring, as he had airily put it, "Not to air our rather grubby laundry in public." He instead brought in two men from MI5's Counter-Intelligence section to guard the Colonel.

The second of the two suited men walked into the drawing room carrying two coffee cups. This one had a similar dour disposition and, although of a similar age to the first, about forty, had slightly more hair and weighed fifty pounds less. "Is he giving you any trouble?" he asked as he handed one of the cups to his seated partner. "The boss said he could be tricky."

"Tricky? He's in danger of boring me to death." Mabbitt pretended not to hear as he resumed his seat and took a drink.

"Well, gentlemen. What should I call you?" Mabbitt asked as he looked into his whisky glass.

"I'm MacIntyre, he's Jones," the second one said as he sat in the chair opposite Mabbitt.

"I see. So this is to be my Tartarus, is it? For the time being at least. Which I suppose makes you two Cottus and Briareus."

"What is he talking about now?" Jones asked MacIntyre with an irritated and mystified expression. MacIntyre shrugged.

"Greek mythology, you know," Mabbitt explained helpfully. "Plato wrote that souls who were judged to receive punishment were sent to Tartarus, an underworld prison, and were guarded by the Hecatonchires, Cottus and Briareus. Mind you..." he added, "they did have one hundred arms and fifty heads each." Mabbitt drained his glass as Jones looked at MacIntyre incredulously.

For the next hour and half Mabbitt quite happily engaged the two men in, what was for the most part, a one sided conversation about mythology and philosophy. Finally the last rays of sunlight disappeared and the time Mabbitt had been patiently waiting for all evening had come. After excusing himself saying that he was off to bed, he left the two men in the drawing room, the relief that he had finally stopped talking clearly evident on their faces.

"What are we doing here, Phil?" Jones asked despairingly as he loosened his tie and put his feet up on the sofa. "This isn't what we do, for Christ's sake; babysitting some old nutcase."

"That old nutcase has been in this game for forty years and is about as good as they come. Don't be fooled by that 'what ho Jeeves' routine, he's got a mind like a steel trap. I checked him out earlier. Most of what he's done is so classified, it's restricted to the very highest level." MacIntyre looked thoughtfully at Jones. "The question you should really be asking is, why are we reporting directly to the Chairman of the JIC? If Peterson has got himself personally involved, well, let's just say we'd better make sure that nothing goes wrong while we've got him."

Closing the bedroom door, Mabbitt smiled to himself, pleased with his performance that evening. His two guards wouldn't now want to come anywhere near him for the rest of the night, just in case he fulfilled his promise to explain to them, in fascinating detail, the subtle variations between Greek and Roman mythology.

Mabbitt worked quickly. Pulling back the Persian rug at the foot of the bed, he lifted part of the floorboard to reveal a floor safe. Tapping in the four digit code on the keypad, he opened the door and lifted out a brown envelope, five hundred pounds in cash and a small automatic pistol. Throwing everything into a small holdall, together with a couple of changes of clothes, he closed the safe door and replaced the rug.

Mabbitt sat for a moment on the edge of the bed and looked across at a silver framed photograph of his late wife. Reaching over, he held it as he had done so many times since her death. "I'm going to find him, Fiona. I promise," he whispered. "I miss you, every day." He smiled a weak affectionate smile and carefully replaced it on the bedside table. Narrowing his eyes, he focused once again on what he had to do. There would be time for him to mourn her properly when this was over.

Picking up the holdall, Mabbitt crossed to the stone fire place on the far oak panelled wall. Taking down a small oil painting he pressed hard on the wooden wall panel on which it had hung. The panel moved back an inch. Instantly a secret door sprung open in the wall revealing a hidden passage. Taking a torch, Mabbitt stepped inside, closing the door behind him. It was cold and the air smelled stale and fusty. Quietly he made his way two floors down the narrow stone staircase and into a secret tunnel under the garden.

As MacIntyre and Jones helped themselves to Mabbitt's single malt in the drawing room, they were blissfully unaware that the man they thought to be tucked up in bed upstairs was, at that moment, twenty feet beneath his beautifully manicured lawn. Mabbitt found the tunnel cramped and claustrophobic, having to crouch as he made his way uncomfortably the two hundred feet from the house. Eventually he emerged, scrambling into a trench that ran across the end of the lawn concealed from the house beneath the thick boundary hawthorn hedge. He stood upright for a moment and stretched his aching back then, turning off the torch, disappeared into the night.

It was eight o'clock the following morning when Jones knocked on Mabbitt's bedroom door. Getting no response, he finally went in and stood open mouthed in the empty room. Hearing Jones urgently yelling his name, MacIntyre bounded up the stairs and appeared in the doorway moments later. "He's gone," Jones said having searched the room. "Disappeared."

MacIntyre sat down hard on the bed and concisely but accurately summed up their situation with two words, "We're bollocksed."

It could be best described as a difficult phone call that MacIntyre had to make to Sir Neil Peterson ten minutes later. The conversation was short, lasting just five minutes. It ended abruptly with an incandescent Peterson screaming, "Just find him or you'll both be manning a listening station in the Arctic circle by the end of the week!"

MacIntyre repeated their instructions to Jones and the warning that went with it. "Where do we start?" Jones asked. MacIntyre thought for a moment then replied, "He's going to need help. Let's find out who his friends are and pay them a visit. We've been given carte blanche from Peterson to do whatever's necessary to find

Colonel Charles bloody Mabbitt."

CHAPTER FOUR

As Peterson slammed down the phone in his office in Whitehall, exasperated at the ease of Mabbitt's escape, an Air France wide-bodied Boeing 747 took off from *Charles de Gaulle* airport bound for Bangkok. In the first class upper deck cabin Harry Grant gazed absent-mindedly out of the small window as the plane banked right and climbed high over Paris. He had descended into a deep and painful melancholia following the death of Roisin. His psychopathic characteristics meant that Grant was not an emotional man. In fact the only emotions he had felt until recently were driven by hate, resentment and paranoia. Incapable of feeling any kind of guilt or remorse for his actions was a positive advantage in his line of work. Of course he knew the difference between right and wrong, but he simply dismissed them as not applying to him. Grant's usual inability to feel the emotions of love and empathy changed when he met Roisin O'Sullivan.

As the illuminated seatbelt signs went out and the statuesque stewardesses with their china doll faces and perfect smiles glided up the aisle, Grant closed his eyes. A slight trace of a faint smile appeared as he remembered how he had been captivated by the girl he would refer to as his flame-haired Colleen from Belfast.

It had been almost a year ago. Grant had taken his thirty-five foot twin engined cruiser from his home on Ko Similan, the largest of the nine Similan Islands in the Andaman Sea, and sailed the seventy kilometres to Phang Nga. This was a journey he made every couple of weeks or so to replenish his supplies, or when he craved some western night-life, and Phang Nga certainly had plenty of that. Invaded by the Republic of Ireland in 1934 to secure its valuable resources, it became something of a sanctuary for members of the IRA who were on the run from the British Government. Although only a small town on the west coast of southern Thailand, Phang Nga had many elements of the Irish culture and traditions. Not least was Maguire's, a small Irish tavern overlooking the sea.

It was a warm and sticky evening. Grant sat at his usual corner table watching the condensation drip down his ice-cold lager. The relentless night-time chorus of Cicadas and the thousands of mating frogs following the heavy rain had begun and drifted through the open window. That was when he saw her. It wasn't her beauty that attracted him, nor was it the way her wet grey vest clung to her body. Although these things appealed, it was the fearless confidence of a predator in her green eyes that had excited Grant. He recognised something in her, a kindred spirit. Few women travelled alone this far south of the country. Those that did maintained a façade to conceal their vulnerability. This girl was different. There was no façade, no vulnerability to hide. She was afraid of nothing and this, Grant found electrifying. He watched her as she walked slowly to the bar and threw down a huge rucksack, exhausted from the long hot bus journey from Phuket. It wasn't long before the two of them were laughing together. The evening culminated with Roisin climbing aboard Grant's boat and sailing across the Andaman Sea to Ko Similan, totally beguiled by the tall mysterious American.

The next few months they spent diving in the clear blue warm Andaman Sea, exploring the coral reefs and underwater rock formations that surrounded Ko Similan. They walked endlessly along the empty white sandy beaches hand in hand, catching the occasional glimpse of a Mangrove Monitor lizard venturing out from the tree-line. As Grant dozed comfortably in his aircraft seat he remembered the time they spent together, almost able to smell the jasmine that grew all around his house in the forest located on the elevated part of the island. Life was good. He was a rich man in paradise with a beautiful Irish warrior who loved him for who he was.

It was just four short weeks ago that it all changed. As his mind wandered, Grant found himself recalling every detail. They had spent the afternoon on the beach. Although Roisin loved her new idyllic life with Grant there were days she felt homesick and longed for the grey skies of Belfast. This had been one of those days. As she sat on the beach absent-mindedly digging holes in the soft white sand with her toes, she stared at the mainland in the distance. "Don't you ever miss it?" she said quietly. Grant sat up.

"Miss what?"

"The..." she searched for the right word, "excitement. The thrill of a well executed operation. The satisfaction of seeing your enemies in pieces on the side of the road." She turned and looked into Grant's dark brown eyes searching for confirmation that he too felt the same.

"No," he replied casually.

"Not even that Det Colonel and his two men you told me about? What was his name, Mabbitt?" Grant leant forward and kissed her, choosing to ignore her questions.

"Let's go to Maguire's? I think you need music and Guinness and laughter."

Personal Retributions

Reluctantly Roisin agreed and less than two hours later they ran giggling like children into Maguire's, both soaked to the skin having been caught in a short but torrential downpour. Conlan Maguire leant on his elbows behind his bar and looked up from a ten day old copy of the Belfast Telegraph, the daily newspaper that was sent to him in batches once a week. Pouring their drinks, he greeted them warmly as he always did, then looked at Grant earnestly. "You've got a visitor, Harry m'boy." Maguire nodded to a blond western man sitting at Grant's usual table in the corner. As Grant looked across, the stranger in his mid thirties unashamedly stared back at him, raising his glass in salute and smiling broadly. Both Grant and Roisin regarded him with suspicion. Strangers were rare here particularly westerners and nobody ever came asking for him by name.

"Who is he?"

"Says he's a friend."

"That's not very likely. I don't have any friends. Is he alone?"

"Far as I can tell," Maguire said conspiratorially, pushing their drinks towards them.

"What do you want to do?" Roisin asked without a trace of fear, excited by the possible risk the stranger posed. Grant picked up his drink.

"Go and talk to him, I guess." They walked over to the table and stood in front of the smiling stranger and waited for him to make the first move.

"Harry Grant, it's a pleasure to finally meet you. You're a hard man to find," he said in a strong Texan accent grinning excitedly.

"Who's looking?" Grant replied as he weighed the man up. He was well dressed; his short-sleeved blue shirt was made of expensive fine Egyptian cotton as were his beige slacks. His fingernails were manicured and Grant glimpsed the 'Rolex' name on the face of the man's gold wristwatch. He wasn't overtly muscular but looked extremely fit and although his clear blue eyes appeared relaxed and friendly, they nonetheless missed nothing. He was dangerous, formidable. That ever so warm and genuine smile concealed something calculating, Grant concluded. Roisin sensed it too. Although she was wary of him, a sudden frisson of excitement came over her. She tingled at the sense of impending danger.

"The name's Mickey, Mickey Kowalski. Take a load off, Harry, you too, Miss O'Sullivan. Let's have a nice friendly drink together." Grant and Roisin looked at each other briefly then sat down. "That's better, ain't it? Now, what shall we drink to?"

"Why don't you cut the crap and tell me what you want?" Grant said with an edge in his voice.

"Straight to the point, Harry. I like that," Kowalski said laughing and pointing a manicured finger at Grant. "It's like this, Harry. The people I work for are great admirers of your work. So much so I'm here to make you a proposition."

"CIA?" Kowalski roared with laughter at Grant's question.

"Jesus, Harry. After what you did to Brad Mason? I don't think the Agency is that forgiving, do you?" His laughter subsided. "There are certain elements in the US government that, shall we say, aren't comfortable with the President's current intentions to cosy up to the Soviets. These elements are very unhappy at the thought of effectively giving up our tactical nuclear advantage for some science fiction 'Star Wars' Strategic Defence Initiative bull. There's something quite comforting about the present offence programme of mutual assured destruction, don't you think?" Kowalski didn't wait for or expect a reply. "There's to be a summit in Iceland in three months' time. Reagan will be pushing Gorbachev to ban all ballistic missiles in favour of sharing research into this crackpot 'Star Wars' programme." Grant shrugged disinterestedly, staring at Kowalski as he took a long drink. Roisin however was intrigued.

"So what would this proposition be?" she asked, barely managing to conceal her curiosity.

"It's Roisin, isn't it?" Kowalski said grinning broadly. "The face of an angel but the heart of a stone cold killer. You've got yourself quite a reputation for one so young. One of the most gifted bomb-makers around by all accounts. Word is you had a hand in that hotel bombing on the south coast of England two years ago."

"You seem to know an awful lot about us," Roisin said, a little unnerved by just how well informed the Texan was.

"The people I represent believe in doing their homework."

"Do these people have names?" Grant queried, lighting a Marlboro.

"I think you know better than to ask something like that, Harry. We both know that I'm not going to tell you." Kowalski eased back in his chair.

"Well?" Grant said, finishing his drink.

"It's quite simple really. During the summit in Iceland we would very much like you to assassinate President Reagan." There was silence for a moment then Roisin giggled excitedly while Grant stared impassively at Kowalski.

"Why would I want to do that?" Grant replied matter-of-factly.

"Other than you can name your own price?" Kowalski said

leaning forward. "It will give you a chance to not only prove that you are the very best at what you do, but to take your revenge on the Commander-in-Chief of the United States Navy who treated you so unfairly. After all, you were only doing what you were trained to do, weren't you? You did everything you were asked to do, every dirty job they had." As Kowalski carefully and sympathetically began to tap into Grant's deep-seated hatred, Roisin watched, transfixed in admiration, as he gently but expertly manipulated the former SEAL with the delicate subtlety of a psychiatrist.

Grant felt the anger and resentment he had for the US Navy resurface and once again begin to torture his psychotic mind. "They took away everything that I was," he said darkly.

"That's right, they did," agreed Kowalski. "All those medals they gave you are now tarnished, worthless."

"They said I was mad, that I was becoming an embarrassment to them, but I was only doing what they wanted me to do."

"Then there was your betrayal by your former employer, Steve Bannon. But, of course, you took care of that, didn't you? A really masterful piece of work. I'm just offering you the chance to make things right." Kowalski smiled. He knew Grant was hooked. Grant looked at Roisin, her eyes wide with excitement and anticipation. "Well, Harry?" Kowalski said finally "What do you say?"

"Harry," Roisin said taking Grant's arm. "Let's do it together. Who knows," she giggled, "it might even be fun."

"There's just one more thing," Kowalski added seriously. "To avert all out nuclear war it is important that you also kill Gorbachev at the same time. This will mask the real target and avoid the inevitable repercussions on the Soviet Union by the US. How you do it is up to you, just make it look like... collateral damage." Roisin laughed in disbelief.

"You're crazy. The political assassination of the President of the United States is a tall order, so it is, but the Russian President as well? It can't be done."

"Yes it can," Grant said, his eyes fixed on Kowalski's. "I'll do it." Roisin's disbelief and excitement bubbled over.

"If you can do this I'll love you forever."

Grant shuffled restlessly in his seat on the Air-France jet as he remembered that night once he and Roisin had returned home. She had been more passionate, more frantic, more alive than he could have possibly imagined. They spent the next few days searching for the answers to two questions, where and how. By the sixth day they had examined all the possibilities and dismissed all but one as either infeasible, impractical or just plain suicide. The embryo of a plan was beginning to form. The first important piece of a complicated jigsaw was required and there was only one person who could facilitate it. They needed someone close to the President, someone on his staff but, most of all, someone pliable. Grant had contacted Kowalski using the telephone number the smiling Texan had given him before leaving Maguire's, and asked him for a name.

Two days later, just over a week after they had met Mickey Kowalski, Grant had said goodbye to Roisin. They had both decided that it was better that she execute this part of the plan. She was hungry to do it. Partly to relieve the boredom she had latterly felt of life in paradise but primarily to prove to Grant that she could. He had no idea that this would be the last time he would see her, except briefly, from a distance, on a hot day in Paris three weeks later. After they kissed passionately in the airport at Phuket, he watched her as she walked confidently through to the departure lounge to catch her flight bound for the United States.

Grant opened his eyes. He was finding it difficult to process the new and unfamiliar emotions of grief and loss. His mind was a maelstrom of painful and conflicting thoughts but dominated by an overriding feeling of hate. He reached into his pocket and took out the empty Marlboro cigarette packet he had retrieved from the bin in Paris. He looked at it. Inside, attached to the lid, barely visible to the naked eye, was a microdot. The cost had been great, but he now had what he needed to take the next step in their plan. The pieces of the jigsaw, he decided, were beginning to fit into place.

CHAPTER FIVE

There were three of them at the meeting on a freezing early morning in February 1986. The temperature had dropped to minus twenty-three degrees the previous night and, by seven o'clock, was struggling to reach minus eighteen. Izmaylovsky Park, on the Eastern outskirts of Moscow, was deserted as the three men walked through the deep snow towards the towering trees of the urban forest. Behind them three polished black limousines were parked in a line at the side of the road, their drivers shivering in the cold as they stood to attention.

Reaching the lake, the three Generals - Yuri Guskov, Anatoly Vetochkin and Nikolai Durov - stamped their feet and rubbed their gloved hands as the biting cold wind blew across the frozen water. Not even their heavy military overcoats and fur ushanka hats could keep them warm. Guskov took out a silver hip flask and took a long swig, coughing as he swallowed. "For the cold," he said, holding it out to Durov. Guskov watched and then grinned as General Durov gasped and choked as he drank the vodka, passing the flask to Vetochkin. "It's Polish, ninety-five per cent proof," Guskov laughed, his breath visible in the sub-zero morning air.

"So it's agreed," Vetochkin said handing back the flask.

"Yes," replied Durov. They both looked at Guskov for his affirmation.

"There can be no room for doubt in this, Yuri. We have to be sure that you are with us," Vetochkin said insistently.

"If Gorbachev persists with this policy of Glasnost of his, all that is great in our country will be lost," Durov interrupted. "We are fighting for Mother Russia, Yuri, and the very fabric of the Soviet Union. Unless we act, your mobile ballistic missile brigades will be de-commissioned in the inevitable concessions to the West. It will only be a matter of time before Anatoly's tank divisions are reduced to so much scrap iron and what's left, turned into nothing more than an annual spectacle in Red Square on Victory Day. Is that what you want?"

"No," Guskov replied. He had spent his whole life in the service of his country and, like so many of his hard-line contemporaries, was proud of its strength and military might.

"We are all in agreement then," Vetochkin said. "Gorbachev must not be permitted to lead our country down a path that will not only make us weak, but at the mercy of any aggressor that wishes to invade our borders." The other two men nodded sombrely. He turned to Durov. "Nikolai, do you have someone in mind?"

"I do have one man capable of undertaking such a task," he replied earnestly. Durov ran the KGB Illegals Directorate, responsible for KGB officers assigned to foreign countries under false identities. As such he was perfectly placed to not only select the right person but have access to unlimited funds and resources for the operation while maintaining total secrecy.

"And you will ensure that there is no connection to the Soviet Union regarding Gorbachev's death?" Guskov said.

"The officer I have selected has never failed me. He is both intelligent and inventive. I have arranged to meet him in Finland the day after tomorrow."

As the three ageing Generals walked back through the snow they agreed that this would be the last time the three would meet until it was all over. Durov looked up at the grey sky as he was about to climb into the welcome warmth of his limousine and called to the others, "There's a storm coming." Both Guskov and Vetochkin knew that he was commenting on far more than just the Moscow weather.

The Imatra Dam towered over the Vuoksi river as the sun began to set in Finland two days later. General Durov had made the short five mile journey from Svetogorsk across the border to the small town of Imatra. Wearing dark civilian clothes and a black fur hat, he stood in the centre of the dam and waited. Impatiently he pushed back the sleeve of his coat with his index finger and looked at his Vostok wristwatch. As darkness fell, a lone figure walked towards him across the dam. His shoulders were hunched and his hands buried deep in his coat pockets against the cold.

"You're late, Major Koskov," Durov rebuked gruffly. "I am unaccustomed to being kept waiting."

"I'm sorry, Comrade General. Your message was unexpected," Koskov replied respectfully.

"I have a task for you. One of the utmost secrecy. It is to be handled with... sensitivity." Koskov was intrigued. General Durov was choosing his words carefully which could only mean that he was going to give him something big.

"I understand, Comrade General."

Koskov had been recruited by the KGB while studying at the University of Oklahoma in 1971. Born and raised in the United States, he was the only son of a Russian mother and an American father, ideal material in the KGB's tireless search during the cold war to recruit US nationals.

Following graduation in 1973, he left the US and began training at the KGB school in Moscow as an 'aspirant' or Iskatel. It was at this point he chose to adopt his mother's maiden name of Koskov and from then on Michael Alexander Johnson ceased to exist.

Koskov became something of a star pupil and after only two years was sent to work in the Executive Action Department. Executive Action, or Department 'V' as it was designated, was responsible for sabotage, murders and kidnappings, referred to in the KGB as 'wet affairs'. Relishing the work, Koskov was stationed at a number of Soviet embassies in Europe for the next six years.

In 1981 his reputation reached the ears of General Durov who wanted him for his Directorate 'S', which assigned KGB officers to foreign countries under false identities. With his background, Koskov was a natural for the 1st Department responsible for KGB enterprises in Canada and the United States.

"How long have you been with the Illegals Directorate?" Durov said, turning and looking down at the river below.

"Five years, Comrade General."

"And in that time you have become my best; my very best. That is why I am giving this to you, because it is going to take the very best." Durov continued to peer into the gloom below. Koskov remained silent. He could see in the yellow glow of the Dam's floodlights that Durov was composing his next words with even more care than before. "Mikhail Alexandreivich," Durov began, turning towards Koskov and looking him squarely in the face. "You are to arrange the assassination of President Mikhail Gorbachev.

You are to ensure that there is to be no, I repeat, no connection with you, the Illegals Directorate or the Soviet Union. You will therefore be required to exercise a degree of...creativity."

Koskov had been trained never to question his orders. That was a fundamental rule of the KGB that he learned on the first day of training school. But this was so huge, so fantastic the words were out of his mouth before he knew it. "Why, Comrade General?" There was no reaction by the ageing General to Koskov's impertinence.

"There are reasons, Mikhail Alexandreivich. Reasons that you do not need to be made aware of. All you do need to know is that," Durov considered for a moment, "it is necessary." An icy wind suddenly gusted up the valley. As the two men stood together on the top of the dam, Koskov didn't flinch, his blond hair blowing wildly as he studied Durov's face.

"What is the time-scale?" Koskov asked resolutely.

"There is to be a two-day summit in Iceland commencing October 11th. It must be done at the summit before it is concluded. I will make whatever funds and resources you require available to you for this operation, but, and this is vitally important," Durov said gravely, pointing a leather gloved finger at Koskov, "you will report to me and only to me. Is that clear?" Koskov nodded. "Good." Durov said, allowing himself the faintest suggestion of a smile. Taking a large envelope from his coat pocket he handed it to Koskov. "Here is your new identity together with all necessary supporting documentation and details of how to contact me." Durov gripped Koskov firmly at the top of his arms and kissed him on both cheeks. "Good luck, Major Koskov."

Personal Retributions

Durov didn't wait for a response. As Koskov watched the General walk away and disappear into the darkness, he pulled out the US passport from the envelope and opened it. He angled it towards the light so he could read his new name and smiled approvingly. Mickey Kowalski.

Five months later Roisin O'Sullivan sipped a tall club soda over ice in Jiggle, one of Washington DC's many gay bars. She had been in the US capital for three days having left Harry Grant at Phuket airport. With a reputation for being the best 'Leather and Levi' joint in the city, this was Roisin's second consecutive evening in the red leather booth opposite the bar.

At just after nine-thirty her eyes flashed to the door as the man she had been waiting for walked in. He looked very different from the smartly suited executive in his early forties she had seen from a distance for the first time the previous afternoon. Clearly trying to emulate the character 'Fonzie' from the TV show, Happy Days, his thick black hair, normally so conservatively styled, was now greased and quiffed. Casually taking off his Ray-Ban sunglasses he, with a hint of self-consciousness, pulled up the collar of his black leather jacket and made his way to the bar.

Samuel P. Griffin had only recently decided to secretly explore the increasingly strong feelings he had towards other men. It was important that nobody found out about his new lifestyle. Certainly not Samantha, his wife of twenty years, who would, without hesitation and probably quite hysterically, take a baseball bat to the more sensitive parts of his anatomy. More crucial than that, however, was that his employer must never discover the truth. As the Senior Assistant to the Chief of Staff in the Executive Office of the President of the United States, Griffin was responsible for White House operations. As such his character had to be nothing less than unimpeachable.

Griffin's was the name that Koskov, as Kowalski, had given Grant as being most closely suited to his requirements. Roisin had begun watching him the day before, discreetly observing the man's double life and deciding how best to proceed. Now, as the last of the club soda went up her straw with a short slurp, everything was in place. She winked at the tall young man in his thirties with the dark hazel eyes and James Dean profile who sat at the far end of the bar. As Roisin discovered the previous evening when she met him, Greg was something of a regular at Jiggle and would do just about anything if the money was right. So when she offered him a thousand dollars to pick up Griffin and take him home for the night, he was only too happy to oblige.

Thirty minutes, and two beers later, Greg was leading his unsuspecting prey out of the bar to where Griffin's car was parked. Roisin had left ten minutes earlier, having confirmed that Griffin was on the hook. As she had arranged, she made her way to Greg's apartment in Dupont Circle and let herself in.

As Roisin waited in the bathroom she checked the flash on the camera she had taken from her string shoulder bag. She didn't have to wait long before she heard the key in the front door lock and the two men enter. Griffin was quiet and reserved but Greg was talking and laughing enough for both of them. Roisin watched through a crack in the door and waited as they stripped each other and got onto the bed. Silently, she slipped out of the bathroom, stood a few feet from them and focused the camera. The shutter clicked repeatedly as Roisin took shot after shot of the two men together.

Hearing the camera's motor and blinded by the sudden flashes, Griffin turned and fell off the bed amidst a torrent of profanity. "Calm yourself, Samuel. We just need to have a wee chat then you can carry on having a lovely time with Greg here," Roisin said smiling. Griffin, overwhelmed with a combination of anger and terror that he had been discovered, made a lunge for Roisin. Her smile disappeared as she kicked him sharply in the testicles, instantly halting the naked man's attack. "Why don't you go and powder your nose, Greg while I have a word with Samuel?" Pulling on a pair of boxer shorts, Greg disappeared into the bathroom, closing the door behind him.

"Who are you?" Griffin said clutching his genitals and grimacing with pain. Roisin's smile returned.

"You don't need to worry about that. What you do need to worry about is that nobody finds out how you're spending your evenings these days. I'll make a deal with you. I'll keep your dirty little secret providing you do a little something for me in return."

"What do you want?" Griffin asked reluctantly.

"That's better. I grew up with two brothers and I always found that there was nothing like a good kick in the balls to make them do as they were told and encourage them to come round to my way of thinking." Roisin smiled sweetly at Griffin who just glared back at her. "You have one week to bring everything pertaining to the Reykjavik arms summit to this address," she demanded, taking a piece of paper and throwing it onto the floor in front of him. "You will wait while all the information is photographed and put onto a microdot then return it before it's missed."

"I can't, there's no way I can get that sort of classified information out of the building," Griffin protested.

"You'll find a way. If you don't these snapshots are going to find their way onto the White House canteen bulletin board. It would be enough to put people off their lunch and you really wouldn't want that, would you?"

Roisin laughed sadistically as Griffin muttered the word "bitch" under his breath.

"You're due to visit the summit venue on August 8th. I want you to arrange a short stop-over in Belfast on the way to Iceland when you will deliver the microdot to me."

"Just like that?"

"Oh I'm sure you'll manage it, or you'll have more than a sore arse from Greg to cope with. Remember, you have one week...or else," Roisin warned, then turned to leave, satisfied she had successfully accomplished her task. "I'll see you in Belfast."

CHAPTER SIX

Having been granted access to Colonel Mabbitt's service record, MacIntyre and Jones spent the morning after his escape searching through it, looking for anyone he may turn to for help. Finally, having concluded that they would have been far better prepared to prevent Mabbitt giving them the slip if they had been given it twenty-four hours earlier, there were two names that kept appearing.

It was late afternoon when their black Range Rover powered up the narrow shale track that led to a small stone farmhouse in the Brecon Beacons. Skidding to a halt in front of the low stone wall that encircled the house, MacIntyre and Jones got out and looked at the run down farmhouse with derision. "What a dump!" Jones sneered.

"I don't remember inviting anyone from Ideal Home Magazine to come and do a feature." The two men turned in the direction of the deep male voice. Richard Jordan eyed the two men suspiciously as he stood at the back of the Range Rover, his thumbs hooked casually on the pockets of his battered wax jacket.

"Richard Jordan?" MacIntyre asked.

"Who's asking?" MacIntyre produced a wallet and held it out to Jordan. He glanced at the MI5 ID then looked back at the two men. "Oh good, spooks. What do you want?"

"We want to talk to you about Colonel Charles Mabbitt." Jordan continued to stare impassively at MacIntyre without comment. "You were in Mabbitt's unit."

"I know," Jordan replied curtly.

"What is your relationship with Colonel Mabbitt?"

"He used to be my boss."

"And now?"

"And now he's not," Jordan said matter-of-factly.

"According to Mabbitt's file you were his best operator. Stuff of legend, so they say."

"That's nice."

"That is of course until you got yourself shot; by the French GIGN wasn't it?" Jones said. "Such a shame, a brilliant career cut short forcing you to end up...here." He smirked as he looked back at the farmhouse. "How is the back by the way?" Jordan began to look mildly irritated.

"Why don't you two boys just get to the point and tell me why you're here? I've got sheep to worm."

"When was the last time you saw Colonel Mabbitt?" MacIntyre asked. Jordan shrugged.

"About six months ago. Why, what's he done?"

"Until last night, Colonel Mabbitt was under house arrest at his home pending an investigation and disciplinary hearing," MacIntyre replied.

"Got away did he?" Jordan began to smile. "From you two?" MacIntyre looked uncomfortably at Jones. "And you think he'd come here? You'll have to try a bit harder than that if you're going to catch him. Coming here is too obvious and, trust me, the Colonel is far too good for that."

"You won't mind if we check anyway?" Jones said going inside without waiting for a reply. Jordan watched him disappear through the door then turned angrily to MacIntyre.

"What's the Colonel supposed to have done?"

"Suspected murder. Together with the small matter of mounting yet another unauthorised operation."

"Perhaps if he thought he'd get the support he deserved he wouldn't feel he had to resort to taking matters into his own hands. You people make me laugh. You want Mabbitt to get the job done but first consider everyone's political sensitivities, say please, pretty please to the JIC and then make sure all the paperwork is neat and tidy and completed in triplicate. By which time it's all too bloody late," Jordan fumed.

"That doesn't give him the right to mount some personal vendetta."

"What do you mean, vendetta? Who's he suspected of killing?"

"The father of the three terrorists taken out during his unsanctioned operation. One of the terrorists appears to be linked to an American hit man Mabbitt seems to be very interested in. A man called Grant." Jordan didn't react when he heard the name. He had been far too well trained for that.

"And the JIC are using it as an excuse to hang him out to dry," Jordan said acidly.

"He broke the rules and we're going to get him. It's as simple as that," MacIntyre replied.

"Well good luck with that," Jordan warned. "I think you'll find it will be anything but simple." As the two men stared defiantly at each other, Jones appeared at the door and shook his head at MacIntyre. "Not behind the sofa?" he said sarcastically as the two men got back into their car.

As he watched the polished black Range Rover disappear down the track, Jordan sat down heavily on the wall and rubbed his aching back. He had taken a long time to recover from the three bullets he'd got while chasing Harry Grant and had removed from his back two years earlier. The gnawing pain of the early months had now been replaced by a constant dull ache that he managed, successfully in the most part, with powerful pain killers.

Jordan thought about Mabbitt and his two MI5 visitors. He had served with the Colonel for years and knew him better than most. He was certain that if Mabbitt felt he had to go on the run rather than stay and face an investigation, then it must be for something very important. Something in which Grant was involved. Jordan knew Colonel Charles Mabbitt wasn't the sort of man to run and hide. He had too much courage, too much honour for that. He looked at his watch, five-thirty, the sheep would have to wait.

The busy Norfolk seaside town of Cromer was winding down at the end of another scorching summer's day. As the pubs and countless fish and chip shops finally closed their doors, the last of the holidaymakers made their way back to their seafront hotels and B & B's. A full moon hung in a cloudless, windless sky and the sea gently lapped beneath the pier. Above the rolling waves a couple's passionate kiss was abruptly halted as the auburn haired girl pulled away shouting, "Who the bloody hell is Orla?" Turning on her white stilettoed heel she angrily marched away leaving the young man calling after her with a futile apology.

Michael Prentiss cursed under his breath as he turned and leant against the rail, looking down at the sea dejectedly. "Why do you keep doing that?" he scolded himself, frustratedly running his fingers through his hair. As he stood alone listening to the sea far beneath his feet, he knew why. It had been six years since he had watched Orla Duncan die in his arms but it felt like yesterday. He had tried to forgive himself for her death and for the most part had done so. The guilt he had felt for so long had now been replaced by something deeper, more permanent. He longed for the time they would never have together. The brief glimpse he had of the happiness they would have enjoyed for the rest of their lives but which was cruelly taken from him was so painful, so overwhelming, it left him feeling alone and empty.

"Cheer up boy, it might never happen," the doorman of 'The Pavilion' said cheerfully as he walked home having locked the doors to the theatre at the end of the pier. Prentiss was too deep in thought to respond. He didn't want to be alone any more. After all, he was only twenty-three. But despite his numerous attempts to find someone, he was beginning to realise that the beautiful nurse from Londonderry he had met a thousand years ago could never be replaced in his heart. He reached inside his shirt and touched Orla's small silver cross that he wore around his neck.

"Miss you," he whispered. Taking a last look out to sea, Prentiss turned and walked slowly home.

It only took ten minutes to walk through the narrow streets from the sea front before Prentiss turned the corner at the end of his road close to the town centre. Half-lit by the street lamps, Daniel Fearnley's funeral premises looked imposing as he approached it. He looked at the building and reflected that he had lived in Cromer for five years, ever since Daniel had invited him to come and work for him as his funeral assistant. He had loved it from the moment he started. Finding the work both rewarding and absorbing, Prentiss had become an accepted and popular member of the town's community.

Following a period of extended sick leave following a serious 'car accident' two years earlier, he had decided to use the time productively and study for his Funeral Director's professional qualifications. The 'accident' was a fiction to conceal the truth of an almost fatal gunshot wound he sustained while retrieving a stolen secret operation file for Colonel Mabbitt. Now he was a qualified Funeral Director having passed his Diploma the previous year. As a reward, and in recognition for his unswerving loyalty and hard work, Daniel Fearnley offered him a junior partnership.

Climbing the steel staircase that spiralled up the outside of the back wall of the funeral parlour, Prentiss let himself into the little flat above the premises. It was just before midnight as he closed the door and saw the light from the living room spilling out into the hallway. Cautiously he walked towards it, knowing that he hadn't left any lights on when he had gone out earlier that evening. He stopped as he reached the doorway and listened carefully. A faint recurring sound came from the living room. Prentiss tensed and slowly peered round the door. The recurring sound was Richard Jordan gently snoring as he lay slumped untidily in the armchair, his feet resting on the coffee table.

Recognising his uninvited sleeping guest, Prentiss tutted irritably and walked into the room. Sitting on the sofa, he kicked Jordan's legs, knocking his feet off the table. Jordan opened his eyes, looked at Prentiss then squinted at his watch. "What time do you call this?" he said using the tone of an angry parent.

"Don't you ever knock?"

"There wasn't any point, you were out," Jordan said glibly "You're looking very casual for a night out collecting stiffs."

"For your information, I've been out on a date."

"With a girl? I mean a proper one that doesn't need a puncture repair kit?" Prentiss chose to ignore the flippant questions and the smirking face of his friend.

"What are you doing here, Richard? Shouldn't you be playing with your sheep in Wales?"

"I was," he said leaning forward, "until I had some unexpected visitors. It seems the old man's gone and dropped himself in the poo again."

"Mabbitt?" Prentiss said, a note of concern in his voice. "Why, what's he done?"

"Not sure yet but it's something to do with Grant. Whatever it is, the wily old sod has managed to escape from custody and disappear off the radar."

"And the police thought you'd know where he was," Prentiss said. Jordan shook his head.

"They weren't the police, that's what worries me. Most plods can't find their own backsides with both hands in a well lit room, let alone track down Mabbitt. No, these were spooks." Now it was Jordan's turn to sound concerned. "Which means one of the intelligence mandarins the Colonel has managed to upset over the years will be trying to catch him ever so quietly and then put his head on a stick." Jordan paused for a moment. "He needs our help, Michael."

Prentiss rubbed his shoulder as he remembered the last time he and Jordan had gone up against Harry Grant with Colonel Mabbitt.

"Do you know how to find him?" Prentiss asked. Jordan smiled.

"Does that mean you're in?"

"It means I suppose I'd better make a phone call. It appears I've suddenly been called away for a few days."

By 4am the two of them had been heading West in Jordan's battered Land Rover for more than three hours. Prentiss was silent. The disappointment of the evening's disastrous conclusion to his date with the lovely Emily had now been replaced by the excitement of embarking on another journey into the unknown. He felt as if electricity was coursing through his veins and, despite the lateness of the hour, was more alert and felt more alive than he had done for a long while.

"So where are we going?" Prentiss said finally.

"The old man once told me, in this game, everyone needs a bolthole; a place of safety. Somewhere that nobody knows anything about, just in case."

"And where is this bolthole?"

"His father owned a remote cottage in Cornwall he used from time to time for holidays and such, up until he died about ten years ago. My guess is Mabbitt never sold it with the rest of the estate."

"And you think that's where he's gone to ground?"

"Maybe," Jordan said thoughtfully. He didn't like playing hunches but at the moment that was all he had. That wasn't the only thing that unsettled him. Prentiss looked across at him. He'd seen that look before.

"There's something bothering you. What is it?"

"I keep thinking about those two spooks this afternoon," he said pensively. "One of them was a real blunt instrument but the other one; he was a cunning little weasel; clever with it."

"So?"

"So if I was looking for Mabbitt and didn't know where to start I'd..."Jordan's eyes narrowed as he thought it through then cursed and punched the steering wheel at allowing himself to be so stupid. He pulled the Land Rover into a lay-by and screeched to a halt ten yards behind an articulated lorry. Snatching up a large flash-light, he leapt out of the car and, crouching down, began to carefully examine beneath it. Prentiss got out and walked round to Jordan just as he was pulling a six inch square black box from the rear wheel arch. "The sneaky bastards," he said, holding up the tracker, its small red light flashing in the darkness. "They almost got me to lead them straight to him."

"Where do you think they are?"

"A few miles back there," Jordan said nodding towards the way they had come. "They'll be following at a safe distance. They won't move in until they're sure we've found him." He pulled his arm back to throw the tracking device into the field nearby but Prentiss stopped him.

"I've got a better idea," he said taking it from him. It only took a few seconds for him to run over to the articulated lorry, attach it to the underside of the trailer and run back. "That should keep them busy for a while."

More than five hours later, at just after nine-thirty, the Land Rover rattled down the narrow country lanes of North Cornwall. Prentiss, having now been driving for four hours, negotiated the tight bends made all the more hazardous by the high hedges that dominated both sides of the little roads. Jordan knew that the cottage was in the Treneglos area near Launceston and a short conversation with Mrs Collingwood in the local post office revealed its precise location.

Prentiss stopped at the entrance to a short private road and turned off the engine. The road, that was little more than a track, gently curved away to the left just revealing the cream painted corner and thatched roof of a cottage. Prentiss began to make his way up the track. The only sounds were his footsteps and the occasional wood pigeon high in the trees which concealed the cottage from the road.

Reaching the door, Prentiss tried the handle and gently pushed but it remained firm. Slowly he walked around to the back and into a small garden. Far from looking abandoned, the lawn was beautifully manicured and the flower borders scrupulously maintained. Hearing a creak, he turned and saw a small wooden back door was open revealing a kitchen. Prentiss cautiously stepped inside. He was barely into the room when he felt cold metal press against the back of his head and the click of a pistol being cocked. Prentiss stood motionless, his heart beating hard in his chest.

"No wonder you don't get many visitors if that's how you welcome them," Jordan said from the hallway door. Mabbitt spun round.

"Richard, my dear chap, what on earth...?" He looked back as Prentiss turned to face him. "Michael, my boy!" Mabbitt exclaimed, visibly pleased to see them both.

"Hello, Colonel. We heard you might need some help."

CHAPTER SEVEN

It had been two days since Grant had returned to his island home on Ko Similan. Having shut himself in the house with a carton of two hundred Marlboro and the two, litre and a half bottles of Jack Daniels Old No.7, he wallowed in his grief. With the heavy white painted shutters closed, he sat alone in the dark, angrily mourning the loss of Roisin. As he stared into the smoke-filled blackness, the phone rang and rang but was left unanswered as it had been a dozen or more times during the last forty-eight hours.

It was on the morning of the third day that Grant was woken from his drunken stupor by a loud and persistent banging on the door. Staggering to his feet, he crossed to the door, his head pounding. The sound of the relentless knocking seeming to drill into his brain, he grabbed the .45 automatic he kept on the hall table. Sharply pulling the wooden door open he recoiled at the intensely bright sunlight. Holding up his hand to shield his heavily bloodshot eyes, he attempted to focus on the white suited figure wearing a panama hat standing in front of him. While his addled brain tried to cope with the affects of the alcohol and the prolonged period of inactivity, he levelled the gun at his visitor's chest. "You okay, Harry? You look like crap." The familiar Texan drawl was unmistakable. Grant lowered the gun recognising Koskov, the man he knew as Mickey Kowalski.

Koskov followed Grant as he wearily walked back inside the gloom and slumped down hard in the armchair. Koskov wafted his hat in front of his face as the stale tobacco smell hit his nostrils.

"Mind if I open a window, Harry?" He said pulling back one of the shutters and throwing the window open. Grant didn't reply as he lit another cigarette. "I've been trying to call you. Thought I'd better come and see if you were okay." Koskov said cheerfully, trying to conceal his irritation at having to make the long and difficult journey. When Grant had missed two scheduled calls to update him on his progress, Koskov had begun to get concerned. He knew of the events in Paris from his contact in the Russian Embassy there. It worried him that the whole operation was entirely dependent on Grant. If he was unable or unwilling to carry it out, it would reflect very badly on him with General Durov, and that was unacceptable.

Koskov sat on the small bamboo table in front of Grant. He looked into Grant's vacant, half-closed eyes. "Harry" he said, but there was no response. "Harry!" Koskov shouted and went to slap his face but, in a split second, Grant grabbed Koskov's wrist, gripping it tightly and holding it just a couple of inches from his face.

"Don't do that." Grant said coldly, unemotionally, his eyes turning slowly and staring at Koskov. "You don't know me well enough to do that." Koskov didn't reply. He knew that Grant was unstable in normal circumstances but he was becoming very aware that in his present state he would need to handle him with the utmost care.

"I heard about Roisin. Sorry, Harry." Koskov said gently. Grant nodded and released his arm. "I know this is tough for you but I need to know that you're still okay to carry on...with the operation."

"I need to know who they were, the ones that killed Roisin and her brothers in Paris. Can you use your connections to find out?" He said earnestly.

Personal Retributions

"When I heard I did made some enquiries." Koskov said. Two days earlier he had made a phone call to a small flat in Islington. It was 5am in London when the civil servant, close to retirement age, answered with his cut-glass English accent. Timothy Haines had spent his career in the Civil Service, first at the Ministry of Defence then later in the Cabinet Office attached to the Joint Intelligence Committee. It was as part of a delegation attending a five day defence conference in Stockholm in 1975 that he fell prey to a KGB honey-trap and was blackmailed into betraying his country. From then on he passed almost every piece of secret information to his KGB handler that crossed his desk.

Now as part of the administration team for the JIC he was perfectly placed to find out what Koskov needed to know. As he sat up in bed, alone in his small one bedroomed flat he listened silently as Koskov told him exactly what he needed. He knew better than to argue, he was in far too deep for that, but he did query as to why the American stranger would be ringing back that evening for the information rather than telling him to pass it on through the usual channels. Koskov's reply before ending the call was sharp and unequivocal as he spat out the words "Just do as you're told."

"And?" Grant said urgently.

"Roisin and her family had been under surveillance in Belfast. As part of that surveillance operation they were followed to Paris."

"Who mounted the surveillance?"

"It was some top secret army intelligence unit commanded by a Colonel..."

"Mabbitt." Grant interrupted "Colonel Charles Mabbitt." He began to feel the rage well up inside him now he had the name of the person responsible for Roisin's death. "Where is he now?"

"Nobody knows. He escaped while under arrest for the murder of Roisin's father. An MI5 team are hunting him as we speak but so far they've had no luck finding him." Koskov looked at Grant. He needed to get the man to focus on the operation again. Any personal distractions couldn't be tolerated. "Perhaps the people I represent may be able to, shall we say, arrange for some specialists to locate this man for you."

"You find Mabbitt and bring him to me." Grant said, taking a long draw on his cigarette and watching the smoke rise into the air, "And I'll complete your operation."

It was almost midnight when Koskov dialled the international number from his hotel room in Phuket. Even though it was nine in the evening, General Durov was still sitting behind his huge desk in his office deep inside the Lubyanka building. Lifting the receiver and hearing Koskov's voice, Durov stopped sipping his glass of hot black tea. "Mikhail Alexandreivich, it has been several days since your last communication. I was beginning to get a little concerned." His voice was without either warmth or expression.

"I'm sorry, Comrade General. There have been complications."

"What sort of complications? Does the American, Grant suspect your true identity?"

"No sir, he has no idea that I am KGB. It is the Irish woman that was killed during a British Intelligence operation in Paris. Although Grant is proceeding with the mission I require your assistance in a small search and recovery operation." As Koskov sat on the edge of his bed he explained in detail what he needed from

Personal Retributions

Durov.

"I will have the two officers from Department 'V' based in our embassy in London briefed immediately. I hope this desire for retribution against this Colonel Mabbitt won't be too much of a distraction for the American. I need not remind you, Mikhail Alexandreivich that if this mission fails there will be consequences…for all of us."

"No, Comrade General." Durov's thinly veiled threat irritated Koskov. He knew that Durov would make sure that any failure was placed squarely on his shoulders. He would need to use all his guile if he was going to survive this, whatever the outcome.

In his office in the KGB Illegals Directorate, General Durov finished his tea as he considered Koskov's latest request. Mounting clandestine operations using agents from the Executive Action Department, particularly in the United Kingdom, was rare. So the kidnapping of a senior military intelligence officer, albeit a disgraced one, that was also being actively sought by the British Security Services was inherently problematic. There was a very real danger of their exposure leading to a subsequent diplomatic furore that would resonate around the world. Durov tapped his finger on the desk as he considered all the ramifications of sanctioning such an action. What concerned him most was that the entire Reykjavik operation would be compromised. He knew that his order to kidnap Mabbitt wouldn't be questioned by anyone involved at the embassy, he was far too powerful for that. It was the certainty that if it came to the attention of central committee of the Politburo, then the whole plan to kill Gorbachev would unravel.

Gorbachev had to die. Of that much Durov was certain.

Koskov's plan involving the American, Grant was by far the most viable. He stared up at the painting of Joseph Stalin hanging on his wall. This, he concluded, was not the time to be timid. As he recalled Stalin's famous quotation Death solves all problems-no man, no problem, he picked up the telephone. The time had come for courage, and, if bold actions were needed, then so be it. He cleared his throat and in his deep monotone voice General Durov said "Get me our embassy in London."

At the remote cottage near the Cornish village of Treneglos, Mabbitt, Jordan and Prentiss sat around a large wrought iron table in the garden eating sandwiches. Mabbitt had avoided talking about what had led to the three of them being reunited, confining the conversation to small-talk. "How's that shoulder of yours, Michael?" He asked as he poured the tea from a large Royal Albert pot.

"Oh you know Colonel. It only hurts when I laugh."

"That's alright then. Particularly in your job. Tell me, do they teach you to have a permanently miserable expression?" Prentiss smiled.

"No, that comes naturally." Jordan interrupted.

"I see you haven't gone stale in your retirement, Richard. I'm impressed that you managed to find me."

"Lucky guess." Jordan replied and looked admiringly at the cottage. "Nice place you've got here."

"Yes, thank you. It is rather quaint isn't it? Mrs Drummond comes in and 'does' twice a week and her husband takes care of everything else. Quite a satisfactory arrangement really. One never knows when one might need a place of....solitude. Speaking of which how are things in Wales? Are you still enjoying the peace and quiet of the Brecon Beacons?"

"I was, Colonel." Jordan said. His tone becoming more serious. "Until I had a visit from a couple of particularly humourless spooks who were looking for you. They seemed to think you might be hiding in my wardrobe." Mabbitt looked at Jordan intently then sighed heavily.

"You two shouldn't be here. This doesn't involve you."

"That's what I said but Michael insisted we come, you know how he worries." Jordan replied. "So I'm afraid whether you like it or not we're here now, so why don't you let us help you?"

"What's going on, Colonel?" Prentiss asked. Mabbitt put down his cup and thought pensively for a moment. It was clear there was nothing he could say to dissuade them from getting involved. And if he was right, their help would be very welcome.

For the next hour Prentiss and Jordan listened attentively as Mabbitt explained, in detail, the sequence of events leading up to his escape from house arrest, beginning with Roisin O'Sullivan's arrival in Belfast. Prentiss was the first to speak when Mabbitt had finished. "You think this girl, Roisin wasn't in Belfast just to build a car-bomb for dear old dad? That she had some other agenda either for or with, Grant?"

"I do." Mabbitt replied succinctly.

"It seems to me the only thing she did that was out of the ordinary was when she went to the airport. So the question is, who did she go to meet?" Prentiss asked thoughtfully.

"It is indeed, Michael. Which is why I paid a little visit to the head of security at the airport when I left O'Sullivan, very much alive I might add." Mabbitt said indignantly. "Having spent a couple of rather tedious hours trawling through some rather dull CCTV recordings I found who Miss O'Sullivan was meeting."

"Grant?" Queried Jordan.

"No. On examination of the passenger manifest I discovered it was one Samuel Griffin from Washington DC."

"Do we know who this Griffin is?" Jordan asked.

"I've made a few subtle enquiries since I've been here with some friends who used to be at Langley. It appears that Mr Griffin is a Senior Assistant to the Chief of Staff at the White House."

"I don't think I like the sound of that." Jordan said ominously.

"Neither do I. What was Griffin doing in Belfast?" Prentiss asked apprehensively. Mabbitt stroked his moustache with his index finger.

"He never left the airport. Stayed long enough to drink a cup of coffee then caught a connecting flight to Iceland. Where he spent the next two days examining the venue and making preparations for the US/Soviet Summit on Arms Control to be held in Reykjavik." Prentiss and Jordan looked at Mabbitt in stunned silence.

"And Roisin O'Sullivan met with this man?" Prentiss said incredulously. Mabbitt nodded slowly. "And three days later she planned to meet Grant in Paris. Why?"

"That is what I intend to find out." Mabbitt said resolutely.

"Don't you think you should report what you know to the CIA or, God help us, MI6?" Jordan said.

"Richard, my dear chap." Mabbitt said exasperatedly. "It may have escaped your notice but I am somewhat persona non grata at present, and besides," he said frowning, "I'm rather keen to deal with Mr Grant personally."

CHAPTER EIGHT

In a small office on the first floor of the Soviet Embassy that dominated London's Kensington Palace Gardens, the fax machine churned out page after page of information regarding Colonel Charles Mabbitt. It was almost midnight on Sunday, 17th August and the huge embassy building was quiet and still. A pair of blue-green eyes scanned the documents as they came through, picking up each page with her long, slim fingers. She was tall, just shy of six feet. Her long blonde hair was tied back in a tight ponytail accentuating her high cheekbones and elegant jawline. Evgeniya Nedelyayev, or, Eva as she insisted on being called, was officially an administrative secretary to the embassy's Cultural Attaché. In truth, she had been a KGB officer for seven years and served in the elite Executive Action Department.

The call that had woken her twenty minutes earlier had been both unexpected and unsettling. She had only met General Durov once when she passed out of the Department V training school. He was renowned for remaining fiercely unapproachable, unnerving both his subordinates and his KGB contemporaries alike. So when it was his voice she heard, as she hurriedly roused herself from a deep sleep, she knew that this must be something of great importance. Durov had been brief and customarily curt. Having given Eva her instructions, he ordered her to discuss the matter with nobody and hung up.

The fax machine finally finished with a loud 'ping'. Gathering the pages, Eva hastily slipped them into a folder, turned off the angle poise lamp and left the room in darkness. Wearing only the dressing gown she had hurriedly thrown on after Durov's call, she padded up the stairs in her bare feet clutching the folder tightly. Arriving at the room adjacent to hers she entered without either knocking or hesitation and switched on the light.

Arkady Furmanov stirred irritably and pulled the bedclothes over his head. "Arkady, wake up." Eva said throwing the blankets back and shaking him hard. He squinted at her and scowled.

"What?" At thirty-four he was three years older than Eva and technically her superior as the other KGB Executive Action officer at the embassy. In reality they had worked successfully together as a team for three years, and there was now little or no demarcation in their roles.

"We've got an assignment...from General Durov." Eva said trying to maintain her composure.

"From Durov personally?" Furmanov said in disbelief. She raised her eyebrows and nodded. "Durov never does anything personally. They say he has somebody to take a leak for him." He noticed the folder. "What's the assignment?"

"Kidnap." Eva said opening the folder. "Of this man." She took out the faxed page of a black and white photograph. Furmanov looked at the picture.

"Who is it?"

"His name is Colonel Charles Mabbitt and he's the Commanding Officer of..."

"The Det." He interrupted. "I've heard of this man." He lay back, folding his arm behind his head, and studied Mabbitt's face. "Eva, this could prove to be something of a challenge."

Personal Retributions

By Monday morning MacIntyre and Jones were under increasing pressure from Sir Neil Peterson to locate and apprehend Colonel Mabbitt. MacIntyre looked wearily at his watch and swore under his breath. It was eight-thirty and he had spent all night pouring through files and records looking for anything that might give him a lead as to where Mabbitt might be. Jones had given up four hours earlier and was now snoring loudly on a small sofa at one end of the room allocated to them at the Cabinet Office.

It had been more than forty-eight hours since they had discovered that Jordan had found the tracker they planted on his car. Having to stand before Peterson like naughty schoolboys sent to the headmaster and watch him explode in a tirade of frustration and rage had irritated MacIntyre. He had been an Intelligence Officer with the Security Services for fifteen years, recruited by a 'spotter' when reading philosophy at Oxford. Having completed rotations in the counter-terrorism and counter-espionage sections, he had now spent seven years in counter-intelligence and was the best they had. To be told, therefore, by the likes of Sir Neil Peterson, who he considered to be nothing more than a jumped up diplomat with bad breath, that he was incompetent made him absolutely furious.

He stood and began pacing, rubbing his aching neck. Jones' snoring grew louder until MacIntyre could stand it no longer and kicked the sofa hard. Jones woke spluttering and scratching his bald head. "What time is it?" He said sitting up and stretching noisily. MacIntyre didn't answer just continued pacing, deep in concentration. "Have you found anything?" Jones queried.

"Jordan must know where Mabbitt is." MacIntyre said thinking aloud. "Why else would he drive three hundred miles to pick up this

Michael Prentiss character in Cromer only to turn round and head back to the South West?" Jones shrugged.

"We used to have holidays in Cromer when I was a kid." Jones said reminiscently. "Is there any coffee?" MacIntyre suddenly stopped pacing. A little bell started ringing in the back of his mind.

"What did you just say?" He said turning to Jones.

"Is there any coffee?" Jones repeated.

"No, before that. About holidays in Cromer."

"Oh yes. We went every year. Dad liked the crabs and Mum liked..."

"That's it!" MacIntyre said excitedly. He crossed to the desk and rummaged around until he found the file he wanted. "Gotcha!" He said triumphantly holding up a faded piece of paper. "Jordan and Prentiss were heading South West when we lost them, right?" Jones nodded. "Mabbitt's family had a holiday cottage in Cornwall and according to this Land Registry document, it has never been sold."

"They're all in bloody Cornwall." Jones said.

"You get the car, Phil, while I brief Peterson. We're going to Cornwall."

Eva Nedelyayev and Arkady Furmanov sat in their silver Rover Sterling outside Timothy Haines' flat just off Caledonian Road in Islington. They too had spent the night learning all there was to know about their target from the information supplied to them by General Durov. They knew, of course, that Haines was passing sensitive information and by 7am decided that it was time to make Mr Haines' acquaintance. Having such unrestricted access to Peterson he was crucial in their search for Colonel Mabbitt.

Timothy Haines folded back the double cuff on his shirt and pinned it together with a gold cufflink. Hearing the time-check on Derek Jameson's breakfast show he turned off the radio and put on his pinstripe suit jacket. His progress to the office was halted by the sombre-looking man and woman standing before him as he opened his front door to leave. Despite his protestations that he was going to be late for work, Furmanov pushed Haines back inside and closed the door.

"Who are you? What is the meaning of this?" Haines asked defiantly as he was forced to sit down in an armchair.

"We are friends, Mister Haines." Furmanov said intently in his heavy Russian accent. "There is something we would very much like you to do for us."

"KGB?" The civil servant said leaning further back in the chair as Furmanov bent over him, his hand resting heavily on his shoulder.

"That's right, Mister Haines." Furmanov confirmed, his face only six inches away from Haines'.

"What do you want?" Haines flustered. He was beginning to perspire heavily. Furmanov took the silk handkerchief from Haines' top pocket and dabbed the man's sweating brow.

"There is currently an operation to locate Colonel Charles Mabbitt by a team from your M-I-5." Furmanov said slowly. "We want you to inform us of any progress they make in finding this man, as and when they make it." Haines shook his head.

"I can't, Sir Neil Peterson is handling that personally. I can't..."

"You will, Mister Haines, or your life will be..."

"I know, I know, or else my life will be made very difficult." He replied breathing hard. Eva leant forward until her face was next to Furmanov's in front of him and smiled.

"No, Mister Haines, it will be very short."

A subdued silence had fallen on the three men in Mabbitt's remote cottage in Cornwall. Having spent the weekend formulating a viable plan of action based on nothing more than a number of assumptions, Mabbitt had come to a decision. For the past hour he had sat alone in the garden, deep in thought, making an assessment based on the scant few facts at his disposal.

"Gentlemen, I feel that we have no alternative than to act." He said walking into the kitchen where Jordan and Prentiss sat together. He pulled up a chair and joined them at the huge pine table in the centre of the room. "Given what we know I feel certain that Grant is planning something catastrophic in Iceland either for himself or on behalf of a third party." He paused and furrowed his brow. "Unfortunately I am equally certain that Sir Neil Peterson will be ensuring that my credibility is severely questioned and, I'm afraid, yours too. Therefore it falls to us to discover what Grant plans to do and prevent it."

"That's alright then" Jordan quipped "I thought it was going to be something difficult." Mabbitt smiled briefly then continued.

"The first thing we need to know is what Griffin passed to Roisin O'Sullivan. That may give some clue as to Grant's intentions." He turned to Prentiss. "Michael, I want you to take a little trip to Washington and have a little chat with him."

"But I don't have my passport."

"Don't worry about that my dear boy, it wouldn't be of any use to you if you did. Peterson will have the ports and airports watched by now. I'll supply you with a false one." He leant forward conspiratorially and patted him on the arm. "I have something of a cottage industry in the attic."

"What are we going to do while Michael's sunning himself in the land of the free?" Jordan asked.

"You and I, Richard are going to Iceland."

"Wonderful" he said sarcastically, "Oh how I love the cold."

"I knew you'd be pleased." Mabbitt smiled.

"The summit isn't for six weeks, why have we got to go now?"

"Richard, just before you left the SAS and joined my merry little band, how long were you in hiding in that Columbian jungle before you put a bullet in the leader of that drugs cartel, hmm?"

"Eight weeks." Admitted Jordan as he followed Mabbitt's reasoning. "But how are we going to get there? Even with a fake passport and a false beard you won't get past airport security."

"You leave that to me." Mabbitt turned to Prentiss. "Michael, come with me and bring your best party smile - we need to take your photograph."

Shortly before 3pm Prentiss was set. He tried not to show the apprehension that gripped his stomach as he picked up the passport and a large bundle of cash. He was clear on what he had to do but the thought of returning to the States made him feel sick. This was history repeating itself. It was two years earlier that Mabbitt had sent him to America to discover who was trying to have them killed. That had resulted in him almost losing his life suffering a near fatal gunshot wound at the hands of Thomas Fisher.

He looked at Mabbitt and Jordan as they too prepared to leave.

He wasn't like them. He didn't have their cavalier attitude to death and danger. He hadn't had their years of experience that had moulded them into the hardened professionals they were. He was glad to be able to help Colonel Mabbitt but, as he thought back to his two previous missions, it worried him that the price he paid every time he was drawn back into their world was getting too great.

"I'm ready." Prentiss said picking up a small holdall. Mabbitt and Jordan stopped what they were doing and walked over to him.

"Don't go talking to any strange women." Jordan said shaking his hand.

"Don't take any chances, Michael. Grant is out there somewhere and we all know only too well what he's capable of. I want you to remain vigilant. Find out what we need to know and meet us in Iceland, understood?" Prentiss nodded. "Good. Take Richard's unspeakably filthy vehicle and leave it at the airport." Prentiss turned to leave. "And Michael, you take care."

Earlier that day, as Big Ben chimed nine, Timothy Haines rushed into his office in Whitehall to the sound of the telephone ringing. He picked it up just as MacIntyre was about to hang up. With his customary superior tone, Haines informed the caller that Sir Neil was unavailable and enquired who was calling. Recognizing the name instantly, and with his earlier unwelcome visitors' threats still fresh in his mind, he told MacIntyre that he was fully authorized to relay any updates that he had.

Having scribbled the details and address of the cottage in Cornwall, Haines rang the number of the contact Furmanov had given him. He felt the knot in his stomach as he hurriedly relayed the information. It was dangerous calling from his office and something he had only ever done once before as the risk of discovery was unthinkably high. Replacing the receiver he stepped away from the telephone taking a deep breath and rubbing his trembling hands together. Only six more months until his retirement. He only had to hold his nerve until then, he thought to himself. Then his nightmare would be over. The sword of Damocles which had hung over him for so long would be gone forever.

Prentiss hadn't even been gone fifteen minutes when MacIntyre and Jones' black Range Rover was covering the last few miles at speed to Mabbitt's cottage. It had taken longer than they had anticipated thanks largely to Jones' skilful map reading. The huge, sleek, black vehicle came to a creeping stop fifty yards from the end of the cottage's private road. Jones pulled his automatic pistol from the shoulder holster concealed beneath his jacket and pulled back the slide. MacIntyre looked across at him concerned. "You've read their files, Danny." Jones said defensively. "You don't really think they're going to give themselves up without a fight do you?" MacIntyre reluctantly agreed. He had always hated guns and up until now, although a trained marksman, had never had the need to use one. As the two men got out of the car and started towards the cottage they were unaware of the silver Rover Sterling that had stopped a few hundred yards behind them. Eva and Furmanov watched silently, intently, with an unflinching stare, and prepared to strike.

CHAPTER NINE

Jordan tossed a heavy bag into the boot of the brown Ford Escort Mabbitt had hired to get him to Cornwall. As he slammed the hatchback shut, Jones appeared and levelled his gun at Jordan's head. Putting his finger to his lips for Jordan to remain silent, Jones then pushed him towards the cottage. With a final powerful shove between his shoulder blades Jordan fell through the door and into the kitchen. "We appear to be discovered, Richard," Mabbitt observed, sitting at the table, MacIntyre's gun trained on him from behind. Having checked that Jordan was unarmed, Jones told him to sit down next to Mabbitt.

"Where's the other one?" Jones asked MacIntyre.

"He's not here."

"He's just popped out for a Sherbet Dib-Dab," Mabbitt said brightly.

"Doesn't matter; he's not important," Jones said dismissively. "Are you okay with these two while I go and get the car?" MacIntyre nodded assuredly.

As Jones walked back towards the country road, Mabbitt glanced at Jordan and raised an eyebrow. He began to stamp his feet and rub his legs. "Do you mind if I stand up, old chap? Poor circulation you know. I'm an absolute martyr to it," Mabbitt said and began to stand. MacIntyre stepped forward and put his gun on Mabbitt's right shoulder to restrain him. Instantly Mabbitt grabbed the man's gun hand and twisted it. Jordan leapt forward and, with a single blow to the neck with the edge of his hand, rendered MacIntyre unconscious.

Personal Retributions

Unaware that MacIntyre had been overpowered in the kitchen, Jones had almost reached the road. He tucked his gun back into its holster as two figures appeared in front of him. Both the man and the woman smiled warmly as they approached. Jones was just about to ask what they wanted when Eva produced the silenced Makarov pistol she had concealed behind her back and fired a single muffled shot. Propelled backwards, Jones was dead before he hit the ground, a small black hole in the centre of his forehead. Eva and Furmanov didn't even break their stride as they continued towards the cottage.

Mabbitt and Jordan had wasted no time and were out of the cottage and in the car. The Escort's wheels spun in the dirt as Jordan stomped hard on the accelerator. He swore in disbelief as the car came under a hail of bullets from the man and woman in front of them. He swerved violently, narrowly avoiding Jones' body. Eva and Furmanov continued firing, shattering the back window and one of the lights as the car reached the end of the private road.

As the Escort skidded onto the little country road, MacIntyre staggered around to the front of the cottage just in time to see Eva and Furmanov disappear out of sight, still firing their weapons. Still feeling groggy, he cocked his automatic and began to give chase. Stopping momentarily as he reached Jones' body, he looked at his lifeless open eyes. Consumed with anger, MacIntyre made it to the road as the silver Rover Sterling sped past him. He watched it career round the bend then ran towards the Range Rover. A bullet in one of the front tyres prevented him from giving chase. He cursed and angrily kicked the flat tyre. He slumped down in the road and leant back against the car. He asked himself the same question that Jordan was asking Mabbitt as they made good their escape; "Who the bloody hell were those two?"

Almost six thousand miles away on the tiny island of Ko Similan, Harry Grant had begun formulating his plan in earnest. Mikhail Koskov, the man he knew as Mickey Kowalski, had left the previous day but, despite Grant's assurances, he still had serious concerns as to whether Grant was stable enough to continue with the operation.

Having taken a long hot shower followed by a short and reinvigorating ice cold one, Grant had shaved and dressed in a clean white linen shirt and chinos. He then sat quietly alone on the veranda and ate some fresh yoghurt and slices of mango, the first proper meal he had eaten for days. As he finished his glass of orange juice, Grant's eyes darted up to his left, attracted by a momentary flash in the densely wooded escarpment a quarter of a mile from his house. He scanned the tree line for a few moments but saw nothing and put it down to a lack of sleep.

He went inside and set to work making prints from the microdot he had brought back from Paris. The information it contained was comprehensive. Presidential schedules, US delegation list and Secret Service deployment and strength together with photographs and detailed floor plans of the venue itself. Grant pinned the floor plans on the wall together with a map of the area surrounding the venue. He studied them carefully. Then, out of the corner of his eye through the open window, he saw it again; a dazzling flash; longer this time and from the same location as before. Somebody was watching him, Grant was sure of it now. He didn't react. He didn't give any indication that he had seen the sunlight reflecting in the lenses of the powerful binoculars trained on him.

Personal Retributions

Casually Grant walked out of the front door and stood on the veranda. He yawned and stretched his arms allowing him to surreptitiously get a fix on whoever was watching him. Satisfied that they hadn't moved, he walked round to the back of the house, disappearing from view. Despite the intense heat and eighty per cent humidity, Grant sprinted over the uneven terrain as he climbed the escarpment. Once he was amongst the huge Ironwood and Gum trees, he began to circle around, approaching his prey from behind.

Grant moved without making a sound. His dark brown eyes stared intently at the figure laying prone twenty-five yards in front of him. The man was slight, he couldn't have weighed much more than a hundred pounds, no match for someone like Grant. Not that Grant would have cared if he had been a two hundred and fifty pound body-builder. Clearly no threat, Grant grabbed him by the nape of the neck and pulled him to his feet. "*Nyet! Nyet!*" the terrified man screamed, dropping the binoculars as Grant gripped his neck tighter and tighter.

"What's that? Russian?" Grant said shaking the sweating, middle-aged man like a rag doll, his wet and matted grey hair sticking to his forehead. Grant threw him to the ground on his back and knelt over him.

"You speak English?" he said venomously.

"*Leetle*," the Russian stammered.

"Who sent you to spy on me?" The Russian shook his head unable to speak. Grant pulled a large tactical knife from its scabbard in his waistband and held it up to the man's unshaven face. On seeing the blade he desperately tried to scramble away but Grant held him firm. "You tell me what I want to know or I'll make sure that you never spy on anyone again. I'll cut your eyes out one at a time." He put the point of the knife under the Russian's right eye and began to press.

"*KGB! KGB!*" he yelled, writhing in terror as he felt the tip of the knife break the skin. Grant stopped. He hadn't expected that. Why would the KGB be watching him? Obviously it was connected to the Iceland job, had to be. But how had the Russians found out about it? As far as he was aware only Kowalski and his American employers knew. The KGB man's tearful pleas for his life irritated Grant, disturbing his train of thought. Almost without being conscious of it, Grant pushed the knife through the man's eye and into his brain, silencing him instantly.

Grant walked back to the house, leaving the body for the Monitor lizards. As he did so he continued to consider how the KGB had become involved. Had there been a leak? If so, it had to have come from Kowalski or his employers. In any event, the Russians now knew of his involvement. What concerned him was how much more did they know and, more importantly, how much would it compromise the operation?

Koskov had sat in silence as he took Grant's telephone call in his Phuket hotel room later that day. His reaction of unease and astonishment was genuine as Grant calmly relayed the events earlier that day, as was his relief when Grant told him, quite matter-of-factly, that he had killed him. Koskov told Grant to continue with the operation and that he would take the matter up with his employers in the States.

"*B'lyad!*" Koskov said angrily having put down the phone, hoping he had done enough to deflect any suspicion from him. It was Durov, Koskov concluded, the interfering old *piz' da*. He could have ruined everything with his meddling. He felt the rage welling up inside him at the man's stupidity. Koskov's anger finally boiled over as he snatched up a vase of flowers and hurled it against the wall with an ear-splitting yell. Meanwhile, in his house on Ko Similan, Grant stared silently at the phone and took a long thoughtful draw on his cigarette.

Having raced away from the cottage, Mabbitt and Jordan had spent the rest of the afternoon in a frantic attempt to lose the mysterious silver Rover Sterling. Jordan had driven the Escort along the narrow Cornish roads with the skill and precision of a top class rally driver. More than once Furmanov had almost caught them, only forced to fall back as bullets screed off their bonnet from Mabbitt firing a volley of shots through the shattered back window of the Escort. Crossing the county border into Devon they dropped down into the labyrinth of tiny roads in the Dartmoor National Park. It was now five-thirty and Jordan had been driving for almost two hours. He and Mabbitt agreed that the only way they were going to lose their pursuers was to head for Exeter.

It was just before 6pm, rush hour, as they drove past St. Thomas railway station and into the centre of the city. In his rear-view mirror, Jordan could see the now familiar Sterling and its two occupants three cars behind. As they approached a large junction the lights changed to red and the traffic began to queue. Jordan decided that it was now or never. Pulling out into the oncoming traffic, he sped through the red light and, with the sound of squealing brakes and car horns blaring in his wake, he left the Rover in the chaos behind unable to follow. Minutes later Jordan turned into the relative safety of a trading estate close to the university.

"Well done, Richard, splendid job," Mabbitt said as they sat in a secluded area behind a huge DIY retail warehouse.

"I don't know who those two were, Colonel but they certainly don't give up easily," Jordan said looking around him to make sure their pursuers hadn't discovered them. "Where to now?"

"Have you ever seen The Golden Hind?" Mabbitt asked.

"No, Sir. My mother would never let me go to places like that," Jordan replied with mock sincerity.

"And to think you used to be my best man," Mabbitt said despairingly. "For your information, The Golden Hind was Sir Francis Drake's ship when he circumnavigated the world in the sixteenth century. It's currently moored a few miles from here in Brixham Harbour."

"Well, Colonel," Jordan said frowning as they both got out of the car, "we can't go anywhere in this. We've already attracted too much attention. We'd better find another one."

"Oh I don't think there's any need for that. We'll take the train. We don't need the plods adding to our problems by looking for a stolen car. It's a shame about this one though," he said wistfully as he looked at the extensive bullet damage. "I probably won't get my deposit back now."

It was ten o'clock when Jordan and Mabbitt stood together on the quayside in the little Devon fishing town of Brixham. Although it was now dark, the many tourists who visited the area, staying at the numerous holiday parks and guest houses, roamed the narrow streets that led down to the harbour.

Gently lit by lanterns hanging along its length, The Golden Hind dominated the small harbour. Surrounded by small wooden dinghies and the larger fishing boats, the galleon's three masts towered into the night sky. Jordan looked unimpressed but smiled when Mabbitt suggested that they go for a drink in the pub nearby.

The Rising Sun was warm and noisy after the tranquillity of the harbour. It smelled of beer and cigarettes and the air was filled with rowdy, boisterous laughter. The walls of the bar were covered with nets and shells and all manner of sea fishing paraphernalia. Mabbitt stood just inside the door and scanned the room until he saw who he was looking for. The man was easy to spot as he stood head and shoulders above the others. Like those around him, he wore a thick knitted pullover, corduroy trousers and wellingtons but topped it off with a green watch cap perched precariously on the back of his head. Mabbitt and Jordan picked their way across the busy pub to the group of men standing next to the jukebox. The giant in the watch cap recognized Mabbitt as he approached and, excitedly excusing himself, hurried to meet him.

Standing six feet eight, the man was almost as huge as the grin that was now spread across his face. Limping heavily, he made his way towards Mabbitt, his massive hand already outstretched. Reaching him he grasped Mabbitt's hand and shook it vigorously. "Colonel, I can't believe it. It's good to see you. How long has it been?"

"Too long, Tug. It's good to see you too," Mabbitt said appearing equally delighted to see the man. Tug looked at Jordan who offered a friendly nod. "Is there somewhere private we can go and talk?"

After having a quiet word with the landlord, Tug directed them upstairs to a small kitchen saying he'd go and get a bottle and join them in a minute.

"Tug Soames was one of my first recruits to The Det. I pinched him from the Royal Marines," Mabbitt explained to Jordan while they were alone. "He was captured by the IRA in '71 during an operation and tortured for three days. When they had finally finished with him they threw him out of the back of a truck late one night on the Falls Road with his kneecap shot out."

"That was him?" Jordan said. Mabbitt nodded ruefully.

"He's one of the bravest men I have ever known. After all the despicable things they did to him..." Mabbitt hesitated. He still felt responsible for what had happened even after so many years. "Once the medics put him back together again he came to live down here." Mabbitt was cut short as Soames came in with a bottle of *Teachers* and three glasses.

"Do I take it that this isn't a social call, Colonel?" Soames said coming straight to the point as he poured the whisky.

"I'm afraid not, Tug. Richard and I appear to have got ourselves embroiled in rather a complicated mess and I was hoping that you might be able to do us a small kindness."

"Anything."

"Am I right in thinking that you still have that huge fishing boat of yours?" Mabbitt asked. Soames laughed as he threw back the whisky in one swallow.

"Well that's not after-shave you can smell on me."

"Splendid." Mabbitt smiled. "Tell me, Tug. Do you happen to know the way to Iceland?"

CHAPTER TEN

It was late afternoon on Tuesday 19th when Michael Prentiss, travelling as Callum Daniels, cleared customs at Dulles airport. Having spent an uncomfortable night on the floor of Heathrow's international departures waiting for the first flight of the morning, he had slept fitfully during the eight hour flight to Washington. With the ubiquitous "Have a nice day" from the customs officer, he breathed a sigh of relief that Mabbitt's false documents had stood up to scrutiny. His plan was simple - get the information from Griffin by whatever means necessary and get out.

Without air-conditioning the thirty minute cab ride to the exclusive Potomac Village was almost unbearably hot. The open windows afforded little or no breeze as the taxi headed West on the Capital Beltway towards the city then over the river on the Woodrow Wilson Bridge.

Ten minutes later, as they turned into Lamp Post Lane, Prentiss told the driver to pull over and he got out. Watching the cab drive away, he pulled his wet shirt away from the bottom of his back and looked around him. Each house in the long, wide residential street was individual and shouted luxury and opulence making it one of Washington's most prestigious suburbs. It couldn't have been more different from the small Norfolk seaside town he loved so much. Throwing the holdall over his shoulder he casually strolled up the street. It only took a few minutes to reach Samuel Griffin's house. Probably the largest property on Lamp Post Lane, it stood elevated from the street behind a large sloping lawn and white stone driveway. Prentiss smiled and looked at his watch, 5pm. Now, he thought as he continued walking, he just needed to find somewhere to kill a few hours then come back. If all went well he would be on a flight to London by morning.

Prentiss found a diner amongst a small parade of shops about a mile from Griffin's house. He had made a reasonable attempt at eating the ridiculously huge meal that the smiley waitress had ceremoniously placed in front of him. Finally he pushed away the plate, sat back in his seat and tried to focus on what was to come. Using threats and intimidation was something that didn't come easily to him. After all it really wasn't required when dealing with the bereaved. This was much more Jordan's forte than his. Nevertheless it was vital that he find out what Griffin had passed to Roisin. If Mabbitt had decided that he was the one to do it, then so be it. It was time to put on the golden armour once again; to become that person Colonel Mabbitt had trained him to be six years earlier. If he was going to do this, he would have to be nothing less than ruthless. He swore under his breath and rubbed his eyes. Not even the endless cups of strong coffee were helping with the gnawing jet-lag. He closed his eyes and attempted to formulate some kind of plan but the combination of tension, fatigue and caffeine just made his head pound. He opened his eyes and took a deep breath. Once again in the absence of any feasible plan, he would just have to do what he always did and make it up as he went along.

The sun was setting behind the tall trees that swayed gently behind the Griffin residence. Having changed his shirt and tidied himself up in the wash-room of the diner, Prentiss confidently strode up the driveway and rang the doorbell. He didn't have to wait long before he heard the clicking of a woman's stiletto shoes crossing the marble hall floor inside. The huge polished red front door opened and a slim woman with the darkest brown eyes stood in front of him. She stared at Prentiss, waiting for him to speak first.

"Mrs Griffin?"

"Doctor Griffin," she corrected rather pompously, already annoyed at the stranger standing before her. Prentiss was quite used to dealing with rude and difficult people and was quite unphased by the woman's icy stare.

"I need to speak to your husband." She looked suspiciously at Prentiss on hearing his English accent.

"What about?" It was clear to Prentiss that this was a woman who liked to be in control and almost certainly wore the trousers in the Griffin house.

"I'm afraid that's confidential. Is Samuel at home?" Prentiss held her stare until she finally relented and told him to come in.

"You can wait in there," she said gesturing with a wave of a French manicured finger towards one of the four doors off the hallway as she walked away. Prentiss watched her disappear then walked into a rather lovely drawing room, relieved that he didn't have to get the information out of her instead.

Prentiss didn't have to wait long before Griffin came through the door. He looked at Prentiss quizzically. "Can I help you?"

"Close the door, Mister Griffin," Prentiss said authoritatively. Griffin began to look concerned and did as he was told.

"Who are you? What's this about?" he said with a tentative smile.

"Never mind who I am. I want you to tell me what information you passed to the young Irish woman you met in Belfast airport earlier this month." Griffin stood in a stunned silence.

"I think you'd better..." he began lamely but Prentiss could see the fear in the man's eyes.

"I think you'd better sit down and be quiet," Prentiss menaced, moving towards him. Griffin stood firm. "Sit!" he ordered "Or shall we invite your wife to join us?" Griffin reluctantly sat on a brown leather chesterfield chair while Prentiss crossed to the door and locked it.

"What is your involvement with Roisin O'Sullivan?"

"Who?" Prentiss bit his lip and stood in front of Griffin. He hesitated momentarily then pulled him to his feet, punched him hard in the stomach and threw him to the floor. Taking a plastic tie from his bag, Prentiss bound the man's hands tightly behind his back as he lay face-down on the carpet.

"Make no mistake, Mister Griffin you will tell me what I want to know before we're finished." Griffin snarled abuse at Prentiss as the tie bit into his flesh. Prentiss thumped Griffin's kidneys causing the man to arch and cry out.

"I'll ask you again, what information did you pass to Roisin O'Sullivan in Belfast?"

"I don't know what you're talking about," Griffin said defiantly. Prentiss cursed him.

"Tell me!" Griffin shook his head. Prentiss was left with no alternative. He couldn't risk Griffin's wife hearing his cries and raising the alarm. He pulled a large plastic bag from his pocket and put it over Griffin's head. Griffin writhed and kicked as he struggled to breathe, the bag growing tighter and tighter on his face. Prentiss held it firm. He watched as the condensation increased and Griffin began to lose consciousness, then pulled it off.

"Be in no doubt. I will kill you if you don't tell me what I want to know," Prentiss growled as Griffin gasped for air. As Prentiss began to replace the bag, Griffin had had enough. He spluttered for Prentiss to stop and that he would tell him what he wanted to know. Crying, he told Prentiss everything from how he had been blackmailed by the Irish girl to steal the summit file, to how it had then been photographed and put onto a microdot for him to deliver to Belfast. Ten minutes later, satisfied that Griffin had nothing more to tell, Prentiss released him. Leaving him with a stark warning that it would be in his best interests if he forgot about their meeting, he let himself out.

As Prentiss walked back to the parade of shops to get a taxi back to the airport he considered what Griffin had told him. The photographer who micro-dotted the information had been particularly interested in the venue layout and its security. It was fair to assume, therefore, that Mabbitt's suspicion of an assassination attempt at the Reykjavik summit was valid. The name Harry Grant had meant nothing to Griffin, nor Roisin O'Sullivan's for that matter. There still remained, Prentiss concluded, far more questions than answers. Both the target and the method were still unclear as indeed was who was orchestrating it. At least he could now discount the possibility that Griffin was part of some White House conspiracy. Reaching the parade, Prentiss hailed a cab unaware that he had been discreetly followed from Lamp Post Lane. As the cab pulled away a grey Ford Taurus slowly tucked in behind, unnoticed.

In a small apartment in Georgetown close to the Chesapeake and Ohio canal, an elderly woman sat alone in front of a bank of electronic equipment. Forty-five minutes earlier she had increased the volume in her headphones as she heard an unknown English voice begin talking to Griffin. She had listened and recorded every conversation Griffin had had since the night Roisin had blackmailed him. Within two minutes she had freed one ear from the headphones and was tapping the keypad on her telephone with a bony finger. She continued to listen to the conversation until a voice answered in the receiver.

"Mister Kowalski, I think we may have a problem."

Koskov had no sooner replaced the receiver in his Washington apartment than he had picked it up again and was dialling. He had only been back for a couple of hours after his long flight from Thailand and was looking forward to a stiff drink and some well overdue sleep. He waited for Simmons, a freelancer the KGB used in the US, to answer. Having recruited both him and the old woman specifically for this operation, he had used Simmons to photograph and microdot the Reykjavik file.

"Get over to Griffin's place, there's an English guy asking about Iceland."

"Do you want me to kill him?" Koskov thought for a moment before replying. It was unlikely to be Mabbitt but he had to be sure.

"No. Follow him and report back to me here." Then added, "and be careful, he may not be working alone."

It was 10.30pm when Prentiss arrived at Dulles airport. He planned to fly to London then on to Reykjavik to meet Mabbitt and Jordan on Saturday. The first flight to London wasn't until the following morning so he had the prospect of yet another uncomfortable night on an airport floor. Clutching his ticket and boarding card, Prentiss slid his back down the wall in a quiet part of the concourse, made himself as comfortable as he could on the polished floor and closed his eyes. He had done what Mabbitt had asked him to do but in the process he felt he had lost something of himself. He had terrified that man to the point where he would have said or done just about anything. What sickened Prentiss most was just how easy he had found it. He himself had survived being tortured twice before by two of the most evil and sadistic individuals imaginable. He now had the overwhelming feeling that, no matter how justified or necessary the reason for doing what he did, he was now no better than those that had done it to him. He reached inside his shirt and held the little silver cross. Worst of all, he knew that Orla would have despised what he had done.

Simmons had observed Prentiss buy his airline ticket and now watched him from one of a line of phone booths. Pushing the dime into the slot he reported back to Koskov as ordered.

"And you're sure he's alone?" Koskov said.

"Yes, Mister Kowalski, I'm sure. What do you want me to do? It shouldn't be too difficult if you want me to take him out here."

"No, I don't want him dead," Koskov said quickly. It concerned him that he didn't know who the young man Simmons had just described was, or more importantly, who he was working for. Whoever he was he knew about Griffin's involvement in the Iceland operation. That was enough for Koskov to want to know a lot more about this mysterious Englishman before doing anything precipitous. "Continue watching him, I'll be there shortly."

The sudden sound of dozens of footsteps close by woke Prentiss with a start. The midnight flight from Atlanta had landed on time and its passengers were wearily making for the taxi rank. As he stretched his legs to try and get more comfortable, two men approached and stood over him. Koskov's piercing blue eyes studied Prentiss carefully. "Excuse me, sir. My name's Dawson from airport security. May I see your passport and travel documents?" He held out his hand and smiled. Prentiss took them from his bag and passed them up. "According to this, Mister Daniels you only arrived in the US earlier today and you're leaving first thing tomorrow morning. Do you not like us here in the United States?" Koskov queried playfully in his Texan drawl.

"It's just a flying visit," Prentiss replied holding out his hand for his documents. "I'm sure you're all quite charming." Koskov continued to stare intently at Prentiss, ignoring his outstretched hand. Prentiss began to feel uneasy as he looked at the two fixed smiles in front of him.

"Would you come with us please?" Koskov said finally. Prentiss' skin began to tingle.

"Show me your identification," Prentiss demanded. Koskov's smile disappeared.

"On your feet, Mister Daniels," Simmons said, pulling a small revolver from beneath his jacket. Prentiss slowly did as he was told. Simmons grabbed his bag as Koskov took Prentiss firmly by the elbow.

"Very quietly, Mister Daniels," Koskov whispered. "Please don't try anything unnecessarily bold. I just want to ask you a few questions about your interest in Samuel Griffin."

Prentiss had no alternative but to allow himself to be taken out of the airport to the parking lot. As they reached the Ford Taurus an American Airways Boeing 767 throttled back above them as it came into land. Simmons opened the trunk and told Prentiss to get in.

"I don't think so," Prentiss said coldly. Simmons raised his gun but Koskov ordered him to wait as they were caught in the headlights of an approaching Buick. Prentiss seized his opportunity. He headbutted the bridge of Simmons' nose and ran into the path of the oncoming car. The Buick squealed to a halt as the driver yelled a tirade of abuse from behind the wheel. As the disgruntled driver drove away, and with blood pouring from his nose, Simmons looked across the parking lot but Prentiss had disappeared into the darkness. He cursed and turned to Koskov, wiping the blood away from his upper lip with the back of his hand.

"What do we do now?"

"We frame him for murder," Koskov replied simply, thoughtfully looking at the photograph in the passport. Simmons looked confused.

"Who's murder?"

"Yours." Koskov tossed the passport onto the ground at Simmons' feet and with one swift move, thrust the long thin blade of a stiletto knife upwards between the forth and fifth rib of the man's chest. As the big man crumpled to the ground, Koskov scanned the lot to ensure that nobody had witnessed him stab Simmons in the heart. He picked up the passport and, putting it into Prentiss' bag, left it beside the body next to the open trunk of his car then walked back into the airport to raise the alarm. Whoever this Callum Daniels was, Koskov decided, he wouldn't get very far wanted for murder. Then, once he was located, there were ways he could find out what he needed to know, before Mister Daniels met with an unexpected, and regrettably, fatal accident.

CHAPTER ELEVEN

It was by sheer chance that Eva Nedelyayev saw Mabbitt and Jordan walk into Exeter railway station. She and Furmanov had prowled the city centre streets for almost an hour before they got their lucky break. Furmanov had stopped the car suddenly in the midst of the Queen Street traffic just long enough for Eva to get out and sprint across to the station.

Having reacquired her target, she followed them aboard the train bound for Paignton. An hour later, Eva got into a taxi telling the driver to follow the cab that had just pulled off the rank ahead. By 10pm she watched them go into *The Rising Sun* and telephoned the embassy to leave details of where Furmanov could find her. Thirty minutes later Furmanov pushed open the heavy red iron door of a call box in Exeter, got back into the car and headed south for Brixham.

When the landlord rang the bell for 'last orders' Tug Soames had taken Mabbitt and Jordan back to his tiny one bedroomed end of terrace cottage. Mabbitt had spent a couple of hours explaining his suspicions about Grant and the events that had lead up to that point to his former operator. Without hesitation Soames agreed to help, relishing the prospect of working with his commanding officer again.

By eight o'clock the following morning Soames had been up for hours. Having let Mabbitt have his bed out of deference to his rank and age he, not for the first time, woke in his battered old armchair before sunrise. By seven o'clock he had telephoned the small grocery store he used in town, ordered the supplies for the trip and plotted the route for the week-long voyage to Iceland.

Jordan blearily opened one eye. He had failed miserably to get comfortable on the small sofa that was at least three feet too short for him to lie on. He sat up and winced as a searing pain spasmed through his back.

"Ah good, you're awake," Soames said cheerfully from the tiny galley kitchen that was located in the corner of the lounge. "Coffee?" Jordan got to his feet, arched his back in an attempt to ease the pain and nodded. He reached into his pocket and produced a small bottle of pills. Soames handed Jordan a mug and watched him throw the painkillers into his mouth and wash them down with a large gulp of coffee. "IRA memento?"

"French police." Soames looked surprised. "Don't ask," Jordan said wearily.

"Good morning, gentlemen," Mabbitt said descending the wrought iron spiral staircase into the lounge. "I trust you both slept well?" Jordan frowned and grumpily finished his coffee.

"Come on, Richard," Soames said slapping him on the shoulder. "I need some help loading the supplies onto the boat."

With Tug Soames' heavy limp it took the two men fifteen minutes to walk down the hill to the quay from the little white painted cottage on Rea Barn Road. From their Rover Sterling further up the hill, Eva and Furmanov watched Jordan and Soames leave, unobserved from their vantage point in a line of parked cars. This was the opportunity they had waited all night for. The silver saloon nosed out and began to drive slowly down the road. Neither of them spoke as they got out. Furmanov turned the brass knob on the front door. Seconds later they were inside.

Furmanov stood silently in the lounge as Eva closed the door. There was movement upstairs. Gripping his Makarov automatic, Furmanov began to climb the stairs. In the bathroom, Mabbitt wiped the last of the shaving soap from his face. As he lowered the towel he was confronted with the ugly barrel of Furmanov's pistol a few inches from his face. Mabbitt immediately recognised him as one of the pursuers from the previous day.

"Downstairs," Furmanov ordered, stepping backwards onto the small landing. Mabbitt had no alternative than to comply. As he came down the stairs he saw Eva. She too had a Makarov levelled at his chest in her outstretched hand.

"Sit," she said pointing to the armchair.

"Is that a Russian accent, young lady?" Mabbitt asked as he sat down.

"Be quiet," Furmanov ordered as he entered the lounge. He nodded to Eva who put down her gun and reached into her handbag.

"Why would the KGB want to kill me?" Mabbitt speculated aloud. "You are KGB, I take it?"

"We're not going to kill you, Colonel," Furmanov said. "Although after all the trouble you put us to yesterday, I'm quite tempted."

"Well if you're going to use this charming young woman to blackmail me in some kind of honey trap I feel it only fair to warn you that my back isn't all that it once was."

"Don't worry, Colonel," Eva said with a little smile, taking a phial of clear liquid and a hypodermic needle from her bag. "Your honour is quite safe. You're going on a little trip. There's somebody that is rather impatient to see you." Furmanov stood behind the armchair and pressed the gun to Mabbitt's temple as he watched Eva slowly fill the syringe. She held it up and flicked it a couple of times then told Furmanov she was ready. As she moved closer, Mabbitt moved uncomfortably in the chair.

"Our orders are to deliver you alive, Colonel, but they say nothing about you being...undamaged," Furmanov said pressing the gun harder against Mabbitt's head.

"Don't make this difficult, Charles," Eva warned. Furmanov grabbed Mabbitt around his forehead, pulling it to one side to expose his neck. Eva located the vein and pushed the needle into it. Mabbitt felt dizzy for a moment, then it went black.

With Mabbitt slung over the powerful Russian's shoulder, Furmanov followed Eva out of the front door. "That's far enough," Jordan said pulling back the hammer of his Browning 9mm. The two KGB agents stopped on the pavement outside the cottage. "Is he dead?" Jordan said looking at Mabbitt's limp body. Eva shook her head. "He'd better not be. Put him in the car." Eva opened the rear door and Furmanov laid him on the back seat. "Weapons." Jordan nodded towards the car. Both Furmanov and Eva took their guns and threw them into the floor well. Slamming the rear car door Jordan ordered them back inside the cottage.

Moments later, Furmanov burst out of the cottage cursing furiously in Russian as Jordan sped off down the hill in their car. He and Eva began to give chase, sprinting after the hi-jacked saloon. Five minutes later Jordan came to a skidding halt on the quayside next to *Argus*, Tug Soames' fishing boat. Yelling at Soames to cast off, Jordan pulled the unconscious Mabbitt out of the car and carried him aboard. Slipping the moor lines, Soames went inside the wheelhouse and started the diesel engine. Once Jordan had carried Mabbitt below and put him into a bunk, he joined Soames in the cramped confines of the wheelhouse. "What's going on, Richard and what the bloody hell has happened to the Colonel?"

"Those two monkeys that chased us over three counties yesterday managed to find us again. They were about to spirit the boss away until I turned up."

"Do you know who they were?"

"No, but they were carrying these." Jordan held out the two Makarovs.

"They're Russian," Soames said.

"I know," Jordan replied. "Worrying isn't it?"

Panting hard, Furmanov and Eva emerged onto the quayside to see the rusting fishing boat navigating out of the harbour. They could just make out the now familiar figure of Jordan standing on the deck. "That's the second time that man has prevented us from taking Mabbitt," Furmanov said angrily. "I promise you, he won't get a third."

"Shit, it's him!" MacIntyre exploded, ripping the page from the fax machine. He hastily read the details and looked again at the photocopied passport photograph. There was no doubt, it was definitely him. He picked up the phone and dialled the now familiar number and waited.

Following Jones' death and Mabbitt's escape from the cottage in Cornwall, Sir Neil Peterson's wrath had known no bounds. Fervent in his belief that the two shooters were allied to Mabbitt and killed

Jones merely to facilitate his escape, Peterson decided that he couldn't tolerate MacIntyre's incompetence any longer. The ensuing high pitched tirade resulted in him being recalled and transferred to the section monitoring ports and airports. It was a stinging punishment for what Peterson considered his continued failure to deliver Mabbitt. Short of being sent to man the file archive, housed in the basement of the MI5 building, this was just about the worst job Peterson could have found for him.

This was his second day in the tiny security office at Heathrow airport. The mind-numbing tedium that stretched out before him was forcing MacIntyre to seriously consider his future with the Security Service. He stared at the grey slate-coloured walls and reflected on the past few days. What he found almost impossible to fathom was how a pompous former diplomat such as Peterson could have so much influence over the career of someone like him. As he absent-mindedly stirred his third cup of tea of the day, MacIntyre could only conclude that it was thanks to the old school tie network that Peterson had achieved so much as it certainly wasn't due to his ability. He was tired and angry at being Peterson's whipping boy and was more than ready to pack it all in. That was until the 'ting' of the fax machine gave him renewed hope of redemption.

Peterson finally answered his phone. MacIntyre just managed to stop the JIC Chairman hanging up on hearing his voice as he explained the significance of the fax he held in his hand.

"Who the devil is Michael Prentiss?" Peterson spluttered irritably as MacIntyre told him that he was sure that this was the Callum Daniels the DC police were hunting for the murder of a former mercenary.

"He's one of Mabbitt's freelancers," MacIntyre said. "There's not much about him on Mabbitt's file except a suggestion that he carried out an assassination for him in Londonderry a few years ago."

"Oh, it's him," Peterson said recalling the 'Eyes Only' sealed file that only he and a handful of others had clearance to read. "I remember now. He was secretly decorated for heroism. And you're certain that this Daniels is in fact Prentiss?"

"Absolutely."

"And you believe Colonel Mabbitt is with him?"

"If he's not, it's reasonable to assume that he must know where he is." Peterson quietly clicked his tongue while he considered what MacIntyre had said.

"Very well, MacIntyre. Get yourself to Washington. I'll notify the Americans that you are on your way. And this time," Peterson warned, "don't muck it up."

While MacIntyre was preparing to fly to Washington, Soames' boat had cleared the Scilly Isles two hours earlier and was heading west into the Atlantic. *Argus* was a twenty-five year old wooden fishing boat that had certainly seen better days. At thirty-six feet long, it was very much a working vessel with few comforts and almost medieval living conditions below deck. Jordan had a severe dislike of boats, even those that appeared to be seaworthy, something he was far from convinced *Argus* was. He hadn't been any further reassured when he had asked Soames' the previous day if there were any life jackets on board, to be told that there might be one kicking about somewhere.

The sea was getting increasingly choppy and Jordan swayed unsteadily as he stumbled into the wheelhouse. He swore as the two mugs of tea he carried sloshed over the back of his hand and onto the floor. "How's the Colonel?" Soames asked as he took one.

"Still out cold. His breathing's steady though and his pulse is fine so I think he's just got to let whatever they pumped into him wear off."

"Have you been with him long?"

"A while."

"I envy you. There are times I would give anything to go back to the job," Soames said with more that a hint of genuine nostalgia in his voice.

"After what they did to you?" Jordan queried earnestly. "Mabbitt uses what happened to you as a stark warning of the dangers of working in the unit. I'd have thought that was the last thing you'd want to do."

"Wrong time, wrong place that's all," Soames said philosophically. "I remember it like it was yesterday. August 1971 and I was on an undercover intelligence gathering operation in a pub in Crossmaglen; what's now referred to as Bandit country. A few weeks earlier, two men from South Armagh had been mistaken for gunmen and shot dead by the army in Belfast. As you can imagine, this stirred up a real shit-storm in South Armagh. IRA numbers grew exponentially and virtually overnight created a climate where local people where prepared to tolerate the killing of the security forces."

"Tug, you really don't need to tell me," Jordan said uncomfortably.

"No, I do," he insisted, "because you are one of the few people that can understand." Soames smiled reassuringly at Jordan. "I was in this pub, The Tin Whistle, a real spit and sawdust hole it was, watching this guy we suspected of being the local area commander. Anyway, to cut a long story short, a group of drunks decided I was a spy and then it all got out of hand. I tried to get out of there but it was too late. What with the drink and a stranger in their pub it was never going to take much. They wanted to believe it, you see. And the seeds of suspicion had been sown."

"But they didn't know for sure who you really were?"

No, but by that stage just the suspicion was enough. So half a dozen of them gave me a good beating and whisked me over the border to a meat processing plant in the Republic. No chance of rescue. For three days they used bats, burning cigarette ends, you name it to get me to admit who I was. That's when they weren't threatening to put me into the meat grinder, of course. Finally, after they shot my knee out and I still wouldn't talk, they saw the error of their ways and let me go."

"Why would you ever want to go back to that?" Jordan asked shaking his head.

"Because I miss it. That's why I'm so grateful to the Colonel for asking me to help you. It means I'm still needed, you see. Still useful."

"That's why you named your boat *Argus;* a guardian always watchful, the unit's motto; a last link to your former life."

Before Soames had a chance to answer, the wheelhouse door slid open and Mabbitt stood in the doorway rubbing his neck. "As you know, chaps, I'm never one to complain but I've been calling for a steward for what seems like an eternity. Is there any chance of getting something to eat on this cruise liner, I'm positively famished?"

CHAPTER TWELVE

Michael Prentiss woke with a start and sat up sharply in bed. It took him a moment to gather himself and, as he looked around the shabby motel room, he remembered the events of the previous night. From his hiding place amongst the cars in the Dulles airport parking lot he had watched the Texan ruthlessly murder his partner. As he crouched motionless in the darkness, Prentiss had felt certain that the man had looked straight at him in the darkness before walking back to the terminal building. He had tried to retrieve his bag but was thwarted as a woman in a passing car stopped and, seeing the blood pouring from the dead man, began screaming hysterically.

By 1.30am, after hailing a cab at the airport, Prentiss found himself wandering aimlessly in Washington's downtown area. Finding himself in Union railway station he looked up at the long list of destinations on the boards. He was tired and was finding it increasingly difficult to think clearly so decided the best thing he could do for now was to find somewhere to sleep. After all, he concluded, he had nowhere to go.

The Classic Motel just off New York Avenue had all the kerb appeal of a fire damaged public convenience. If it employed a cleaner it was clear by the condition of the room that her heart really wasn't in it. It smelled of damp and body odour and the carpet, such as it was, stuck to Prentiss' shoes. But it was cheap and the unshaven character behind the desk didn't ask any questions. Without undressing, Prentiss had lain down on the stained bedspread, closed his eyes and within a few minutes had gone to sleep.

In the absence of any hot, Prentiss splashed cold water

repeatedly on his face from the small cracked hand basin in the bathroom and thought about the Texan and his partner at the airport. Initially considering the possibility that they were FBI or Secret Service, he quickly discounted it, concluding the thought that they would murder their own people was preposterous. Nevertheless they did know that he had seen Griffin and where to find him at the airport. He stared at his reflection in the mirror as he turned it over in his mind. The only logical assumption was that they were in some way connected to Roisin and Grant. In which case Griffin was being watched to ensure he kept his mouth shut about his involvement. What Prentiss couldn't understand was why, whoever they were, would the Texan kill his own man?

The answer to that question became all too apparent an hour later as he walked down Pennsylvania Avenue amid the mid morning bustle. Passing a news stand, Prentiss glanced across at the copies of *The Washington Post* and swore under his breath. On the front page beneath the headline 'HAVE YOU SEEN THIS MAN?' was his passport photograph. A smaller picture of the Texan's partner was further down the page. Prentiss read just enough to learn that he was wanted for the man's murder before he realised that he was attracting the stand owner's attention.

It was Koskov's masterful manipulation of the previous night's events that led to the front page headlines that Prentiss now saw. While Prentiss had made good his escape in a cab, Koskov had returned to the terminal building at Dulles and raised the alarm. He had spent an hour giving a statement to the police about witnessing the brutal and senseless slaying of the innocent bystander in the parking lot. A patrol car had even driven him home to his

Georgetown apartment to thank him for his co-operation. Once there, Koskov had taken a copy of Dostoevsky's *Crime and Punishment* from the shelf. Secreted within its pages, written in a double transposition cipher, was a list of KGB sleepers in Washington. Taking a pencil and notepad, he decrypted the name in the police department, Stella Wiseman. It wasn't long before his telephone call woke her. Using the activation code word 'Restitution', Koskov instructed her to inform him of any and all information pertaining to the hunt for the murderer, Callum Daniels. The gravity of his situation weighed heavily on him as he replaced the receiver. Koskov knew that he had to question this Daniels to determine that the integrity of the operation remained intact. Once that was confirmed, he could kill him.

Prentiss walked away from the news stand with his head down, rubbing his forehead to conceal his face. His bad situation had just got considerably worse. Not enough that he didn't have his passport and couldn't get home; now, it appeared, he was being sought for murder as well. He went into a large shopping mall which mercifully was busy, allowing him to blend into the crowd. Buying a red *Nationals* baseball cap, Prentiss put it on and pulled the peak down. Suddenly feeling very exposed, he ducked into a coffee shop and sat in a booth that at least afforded him a degree of privacy.

Ordering a coffee in his best attempt at an American accent, Prentiss sat with his head down and stirred it slowly. He had to think. There was no way he could allow himself to be caught. He was travelling under a false name on, what the authorities must now know, was a forged passport. Nobody would believe that he was innocent of murdering the so called 'innocent bystander' at the airport.

"Well done, Michael, you're really in the shit this time," Prentiss mumbled angrily to himself. This was different to Londonderry six years ago. Then it was just a case of managing not to get caught long enough to be extracted. This time he had no-one to come to his rescue. He was completely alone with no way of getting home. He rebuked himself. This wasn't the time to start being maudlin and wallowing in self-pity. "Come on, Michael. Think!" he whispered getting more and more frustrated. He took a deep calming breath. "What would Richard do?" he thought, trying to focus his mind. Prentiss recalled the many conversations he and Jordan had had about Jordan's military career. He tried to remember one of the many drunken nights at his farmhouse in Wales when Jordan told him about 'Moscow Rules'. These were precepts developed during the cold war for western spies operating in Moscow but the principals were sound and could be applied anywhere. He went through them in his mind.

Assume nothing

Go with the flow

Build in opportunity, but use it sparingly

Keep your options open

Follow your instinct, it's your operational antennae

Prentiss closed his eyes as he remembered more of the list. The one thing he did have six years ago was Orla, he thought. Without her help it would have been very different. Here, now, he didn't have a single friend. He stopped stirring his coffee and slowly opened his eyes. Perhaps that wasn't strictly true. Maybe there was someone. A glimmer of hope began to form in his mind. It was just possible that all was not lost after all.

It was getting hot and sticky as it approached midday in the US capital. Prentiss leant casually in a doorway in the financial district of Minnesota Avenue South-East reading a magazine. For the last fifteen minutes he had watched cabs and chauffeur driven limousines pull up and expensively suited figures get out and enter the banks and accounting buildings close by.

Prentiss knew he needed a new identity if he was going to have any chance of evading the police. He smiled as just what he was looking for stepped out of a cab not twenty feet from where he was standing. Although a little older, about thirty, the fierce looking man with the slicked back hair and Mediterranean suntan was a close enough match. Prentiss watched him carefully as he sneered a disparaging comment then contemptuously threw a twenty dollar bill at the driver and replaced his wallet in the inside pocket of his hand made Italian jacket.

"You'll do nicely," Prentiss said and started towards him pretending to be still engrossed in the magazine.

"You idiot!" the man yelled angrily as, moments later, Prentiss 'accidentally' barged into him sending the American, his briefcase and Filofax skidding across the sidewalk. Apologising profusely, Prentiss manhandled him to his feet to be furiously pushed away. Still apologising, Prentiss walked away leaving the now somewhat dishevelled individual hurling a torrent of abuse after him.

In the empty men's room of a department store, Prentiss wedged the door shut and examined the contents of the wallet he had successfully lifted twenty minutes earlier. In addition to the five hundred and fifty dollars in cash, half of which he had just spent in the store, he had relieved Mario Danetti of his driver's licence and three credit cards. He decided that he didn't need to change his appearance radically. Just enough to look less like the terrible photo Mabbitt had taken of him and more like the obnoxious Mister Danetti. Prentiss looked at the small photograph in the left hand corner of the driver's licence then at his reflection in the mirror. "Shouldn't be too difficult," he thought to himself.

Taking the bottle of gel from the one of the store bags, he smeared two large handfuls onto his hair. He then combed it straight back until it matched the photograph. As Prentiss stripped and put on the new shirt and tie, somebody tried the men's room door. "It's closed for cleaning. Come back in ten minutes," he called in his improving accent. The disgruntled shopper went away grumbling and Prentiss finished dressing in a silver-grey suit. Putting on the new sunglasses, he checked himself in the mirror. Satisfied that he had changed his appearance sufficiently, he bundled his old clothes into the bag and pushed it through the flip lid of the bin. He took a final look in the mirror and nodded. He was ready.

In Union station an hour later Prentiss held his breath as he listened to the ringing at the other end of the phone. Having been connected by the operator he now stood in a phone booth amid the noise and chaos of hundreds of people in transit. Finally the ringing was replaced by a familiar voice. He kept the conversation brief. Uniformed police officers patrolled the station stopping at random anyone that matched Callum Daniels' description. "Thank you. I wouldn't ask this of you," Prentiss said, "but you really are my only hope. My train arrives at a little after midnight. I'll see you then."

On reaching the platform Prentiss found his Amtrak train was preparing to depart. He joined the line of a dozen or so boarding his railcar. A guard checked the tickets as each passenger boarded watched by a DC cop, his hand resting casually on his holstered gun. Prentiss looked uneasy as he got nearer to them. "Just keep calm," he told himself. He handed the guard his ticket and smiled. The policeman stared at him intently, looked down at a clipboard then back to Prentiss. "Do you have any ID, sir?" he said stepping forward and taking the ticket from the guard. Prentiss fought to control his breathing.

"Driver's licence okay?" He reached inside his jacket and handed it over. "This is the third time I've been asked to show that today," Prentiss quipped. The cop didn't reply.

"What's the reason for your journey, Mister Danetti?" Before Prentiss could reply a commotion further down the platform diverted the policeman's attention. A scruffy looking twenty-something was yelling in an English accent at two more cops, furious at being stopped yet again. The policeman hastily handed the documents back to Prentiss and ran to their assistance. Before he had reached them, Prentiss was on the train.

In the dining car four hours later Prentiss finished a large plate of ham and eggs. Growing increasingly uncomfortable and not having eaten since the previous day, he had decided to leave the relative security of his window seat and take a chance on being recognised. On the way he had reapplied the gel to his hair in the bathroom and reluctantly removed his sunglasses. It was two hours until he would arrive in Boston. There he had a further two hour wait for his connection to continue his journey although he thought it was unlikely that the police would be searching for him there and he could relax a little.

At 8.03pm the Amtrak pulled into Boston's South station. Sure enough, just as Prentiss had suspected, as he made his way along the concourse he felt completely anonymous. Having spent a couple of hours just wandering the city, he returned to the station. Giving a last look around him to confirm that he was safe, he boarded the train. Sitting back in his seat as it was about to pull out of the station, Prentiss was unaware of the three suited men sprinting down the platform and jumping aboard his train, four cars in front. The doors closed behind them.

"Prentiss may be alone, or with these two men." The two FBI agents looked at the photos of Mabbitt and Jordan and nodded. "Don't underestimate this man. He is extremely dangerous." The third man's English voice was determined and authoritative. MacIntyre had arrived in Washington nine hours earlier and had been met by the two Feds at the airport. At Sir Neil Peterson's request, responsibility for the search for Prentiss had been handed over to the FBI. It was only thanks to the diligence of the cop at Union station that MacIntyre had been led to Boston. Recognising the name Mario Danetti on a stolen wallet report, he had raised the alarm having remembered the destination on the rail ticket.

MacIntyre slowly began to lead the two men down the train, scrutinizing each passenger's face carefully. They reached the end of the first car and moved into the second. In his window seat, Prentiss began to doze having ninety minutes until he reached his destination. MacIntyre was now entering the third car. The three paused momentarily as MacIntyre looked more closely at a man chatting to a pretty girl up ahead. Satisfied that it wasn't Prentiss they continued forward.

Prentiss was seated towards the rear of the fourth car. As the electric door 'swished' open and MacIntyre stepped in, a hugely obese, middle-aged woman squeezed herself out of the lavatory cubicle in front of him. Filling the aisle, she prevented MacIntyre and the other two men getting past as she, gripping a large carpet bag, tried to leave the car. "Madam, would you kindly move!" MacIntyre said loudly. Prentiss opened his eyes at the sound of the English accent. He peered over the seat in front at the three men. They had to be coming for him, he thought. He cursed, got out of his seat and walked down the aisle to the far door. "That's him!" MacIntyre shouted seeing Prentiss disappear out of the car. Indignantly the fat woman stood her ground, demanding the men back up to allow her to pass. "Just get out of the way, you stupid woman!" MacIntyre yelled attempting to barge passed her.

Prentiss had reached the end of the fifth car and into the sixth. He knew that he was in serious trouble. It wouldn't be long before he ran out of train. Into the seventh car. Reaching the far end he was confronted with a sign on the door - BAGGAGE CAR-NO ADMITTANCE. He turned and looked back down the railcar. No sign of his pursuers although it must only be a matter of moments before they would appear.

Sitting in a window seat a few feet away, a man was talking loudly on a cellular phone. Prentiss thought for a moment then took the empty seat next to him. "Do you mind if I borrow your phone? It's an emergency," Prentiss interrupted.

"Beat it, buddy," he replied dismissively before returning to his conversation. Prentiss looked at him for a second then whipped his bent elbow sideways, striking the man's temple. Letting out a faint cry he fell unconscious against the window. Prentiss grabbed the large, heavy phone and began tapping the numbered keys as he pulled open the door to the baggage car.

Unable to control his frustration any longer, MacIntyre had pushed the fat woman back into the lavatory cubicle and was now running down the train with the two Feds close behind. Seeing the door to the baggage car open, they ran past the unconscious passenger. Drawing their handguns they cautiously went inside. Crouching behind a pile of suitcases and transit boxes, Prentiss whispered into the phone, "I've been found. I'm just north of Merrimack."

"Michael Prentiss!" MacIntyre called from the doorway. "You've got nowhere to go. Give yourself up." Prentiss hung up the phone and crawled unobserved to the side loading door. He tried to swallow but his mouth was too dry. He only had one option. The three men began to move closer. They would find him in the next few seconds. It had to be now. Prentiss heaved at the loading door, sliding it open. There was a deafening rush of air taking his breath away. He stood briefly in the doorway, stunned at the speed the countryside was hurtling passed him. MacIntyre's shouts to stop were lost amid the noise. This was going to hurt, Prentiss thought. Then, taking a deep breath, he jumped.

CHAPTER THIRTEEN

"How much longer are we going to be stuck on this bloody tub, Colonel? It's been four days," Jordan moaned as he and Mabbitt were being rolled from side to side in the small cabin below deck.

"According to Tug, another two days I'm afraid, Richard. Maybe longer if this doesn't improve." They listened to the torrential rain beating down on the rocking vessel. The weather conditions had got steadily worse during the past two days making their progress north slow and laborious. Jordan sighed heavily.

"I don't know if I can take two more days of Tug's frozen beefburgers. Not to mention the overwhelming stink of dead fish everywhere."

"Yes, I have to admit, it is rather pungent," Mabbitt agreed.

"He could do with a pig as an air freshener in here if you ask me." Mabbitt chose to ignore the man's grumbling so Jordan changed the subject. "Any more thoughts on your Russian friends?" he asked trying to wedge himself against the bulkhead to stop being jolted and thrown around.

"No," Mabbitt said pensively. "I haven't had much to do with the Russians over the years; certainly not the KGB. I had a bit of a run-in with the GRU in Berlin in sixty-eight when one of their officers defected and hopped over the wall. It can't be anything to do with him though. He died of a heart attack five years later in Eastbourne. Anyway, kidnap isn't their style. This has got KGB Executive Action Department written all over it."

"So it's got to be Iceland."

"Oh, without a doubt. That is of course providing our assumption about an assassination attempt is correct. Hopefully

Michael's little chat with Mister Griffin will clarify the situation." Mabbitt stroked his moustache thoughtfully.

"What?"

"We're missing something, Richard. Samuel Griffin is linked to Roisin O'Sullivan. Who in turn is linked to Harry Grant."

"Who we believe is going to make a hit at the summit."

"But who is the target? And who is orchestrating it? My guess is it isn't Grant."

"The Russians?" Jordan said. "From what I've seen of Grant I can't see him doing anything as unpatriotic as freelancing for the KGB."

"Nevertheless the KGB do appear to be quite heavily involved. I just don't know who in the KGB would want to go to such lengths to capture me."

"Perhaps Peterson actually works for the Russians," Jordan said glibly. Mabbitt remained silent. The thought that the chairman of the JIC had snow on his boots was ridiculous but, he thought to himself, he had been wrong about people before.

"We've got a problem," Tug announced appearing in the doorway and pulling off his dripping green woollen hat. "There's a storm coming in from the west that's going to hit us in a couple of hours."

"Worse than this?" Jordan said incredulously.

"A lot worse." He turned to Mabbitt. "I'm sorry, Colonel. We've got to put in somewhere and sit it out."

"Where are we?" Mabbitt asked.

"Ten miles south west of the Outer Hebrides. Stornoway has the only harbour but I'd rather not take us there. We may attract some unwelcome attention from the port authorities. They can ask some very impertinent questions at the same time they are taking your boat apart."

"We're in your hands, Tug. What do you suggest?"

"The charts show a small bay on the eastern side of the south Island. We should be safe enough there." He disappeared momentarily then his head appeared again. "We should drop anchor in about an hour then I'll get us something to eat. Beefburgers okay?"

Five miles astern of the *Argus*, a large cabin cruiser, buffeted by the waves, kept pace with the fishing boat. In addition to its two man crew, Eva Nedelyayev and Arkady Furmanov watched Soames' vessel turn hard to starboard. "At last," Furmanov said as the crewman behind the wheel surmised that they must be heading for port. The two KGB officers had followed them from Devon having paid double to charter the cruiser with no questions asked. Furmanov was determined to take Mabbitt prisoner and kill the bodyguard who had successfully thwarted their attempt in Brixham. Although Furmanov would quite happily have contacted one of the Soviet 'Victor' class attack submarines that patrolled the North Atlantic and had the fishing boat blown out of the water, such had been his anger for their first day at sea.

Although it was late afternoon in the small cove where the *Argus* had dropped anchor it was shrouded in an all-pervasive murky grey gloom. Affording some shelter from the oncoming storm, the fishing boat continued to rise and fall on the increasing swell that was whipped up by the strengthening wind and teeming rain.

Scanning the craggy coastline interspersed with narrow strips of beach, Soames spotted a crofter's cottage standing alone on grassland a few hundred yards from a stretch of sand. Suggesting to Mabbitt and Jordan that they may be more comfortable riding out the storm surrounded by four walls, he prepared the small dinghy for them to row ashore.

Choosing to remain aboard the *Argus* to ensure she wasn't swept onto the rocks, Soames watched his passengers reach the shore. Using his binoculars, he followed their progress up the gentle incline to the long, low-slung building. Such was his concentration on the shoreline, Soames was unaware of the cabin cruiser coming around the headland behind him.

Jordan pushed open the heavy door. Even though the cottage was dark inside and had clearly been derelict for quite some time, he didn't mind a bit. It was dry, the floor didn't move and there was a distinct absence of anything that remotely smelled of fish. With the walls made of granite four feet thick, the air, although fusty, was still and surprisingly warm. He dropped the heavy bag on the rickety wooden table.

"This is rather quaint," Mabbitt said as he switched on the large battery operated lantern he had brought from the *Argus*.

"It's certainly better than being cooped up aboard *The Flying Dustman*," Jordan replied dryly.

"Richard, I haven't thanked you for what you and Michael are doing for me. I very much appreciate your help in all of this." Mabbitt was suddenly interrupted by the sound of a huge explosion booming across the small bay. Without hesitating, Jordan snatched an Armalite rifle from the bag and followed Mabbitt outside. The

Argus was ablaze. The strengthening wind blew acrid black smoke out across the headland while the cabin cruiser circled the stricken vessel at a safe distance.

"It looks like we've got company, Colonel," Jordan said seeing the now familiar figures of Furmanov and Nedelyayev making their way towards them from the shoreline. Mabbitt looked down at them angrily as Soames' fishing boat exploded again. Jordan took a last look at their heavily armed adversaries before slamming the door. "Do you think they've got Tug on the other boat?" Mabbitt didn't reply as he concentrated on loading the Browning 9mm from the bag. He knew it was unlikely that Tug Soames would have been taken willingly and would have resisted any attempt they made to do so.

Furmanov and Nedelyayev crouched behind rocks at the top of the incline at the edge of the grassland. There were seventy-five yards of open killing ground between them and the cottage. Pulling back the bolts on their Skorpion machine pistols, Furmanov and Eva fired a short burst at the door. Inside the cottage the bullets ripped through the splintering wood. Mabbitt and Jordan braced themselves, their backs pressed against the thick impenetrable granite walls, standing either side of the door. Jordan flung open the small window and returned fire with three bursts of three rounds from his Armalite. They pinged off the rocks as Furmanov and Eva took cover.

"Colonel Mabbitt!" Furmanov yelled. "Give yourself up and we'll allow your friend in there to live. If not, I assure you we will come and take you by force and put your attack dog down in the process!"

"And my man on the fishing boat, what have you done with

him?!"

"Unconscious but alive. For the moment at least. How long he remains that way is up to you!"

Inside the cottage, Mabbitt furrowed his brow. "Tug's dead," he said resignedly.

"I know," Jordan said maintaining his vigil through the small window. "It's getting dark out there. Another thirty minutes and we won't be able to see them coming."

"If you were them, Richard what would you do?"

"Wait until dark then toss in a couple of smoke grenades," Jordan replied authoritatively. Mabbitt nodded in agreement.

"And is your assessment that they will have smoke grenades?"

Jordan thought for a moment. "They seem to be very well prepared and I don't suppose they've got packed lunches in those backpacks. So yes; probably." Mabbitt remained silent. "Who is so desperate to get hold of you, Colonel?"

"I suppose there's only one way to find out," Mabbitt said moving to the door. Jordan grabbed his arm.

"What do you think you're doing?" Jordan said pulling him back.

"The only reason those two are out there is to capture me alive. Once they have succeeded in doing that you can get to Iceland unhindered and stop Grant doing whatever it is he's going to do."

"Oh, you think they're just going to let me go, do you?"

"Of course not, my dear chap. I'm sure they want to kill you mercilessly. Particularly after you upset their apple cart in Brixham. No, you are going to climb out of that window at the back and scurry off and hide until we've gone."

"And I'm supposed to just watch and let you martyr yourself? I don't think so, Colonel."

"Richard, listen to me. If you don't get to Iceland all that we've done thus far will count for nothing. In all these years you have never disobeyed one of my orders and I'm not about to let you start now."

"With the greatest of respect, sir, bollocks to your orders. I'm not going to leave you," Jordan said vehemently. Mabbitt allowed himself a smile.

"Why is it that when you begin a sentence with the greatest of respect you end it being quite the opposite? You're a good man, Richard. I need you to finish this for me, Michael can't do it alone."

"Are you sure about this?"

"Those two aren't going to kill me, and to be frank I'm rather intrigued to meet whoever has sent them. Now, be a good chap and bugger off." Jordan took the handgun from Mabbitt and, collecting the bag, opened the window on the back wall. "One more thing," Mabbitt said as Jordan climbed out of the window. "Whatever happens in Iceland, I want your word you'll kill Grant for me." Jordan responded with a sharp, stone-faced nod then disappeared.

Mabbitt gave Jordan a couple of minutes to get clear then called out that he was giving himself up. Cautiously Eva and Furmanov walked towards him as he stepped out from the cottage. With their weapons trained on him, Eva stood guard as Furmanov pushed Mabbitt to the ground and searched him. Then, with Mabbitt handcuffed face down on the grass, they both burst into the cottage spraying the interior with bullets. Finding the cottage empty, they returned outside to where Mabbitt was laying.

"Where's your nasty little dog, Colonel?" Furmanov hissed

pulling Mabbitt's head up by the hair.

"I'm most awfully sorry but I'm afraid I don't know who you mean. I don't have a dog. I did have a cat once..."

"Enough! Where is the man you were with?" He punched Mabbitt hard in the kidneys. From his position fifty yards away, concealed in the scrubland, Jordan watched silently. Furmanov grew more and more angry as Mabbitt refused to tell him. Finally Furmanov's frustration could no longer be contained and he fired a long burst in an arc into the darkness. Jordan lay flat as a couple of the bullets embedded themselves in the ground perilously close to his head.

"Arkady!" Eva yelled as he emptied the Skorpion's magazine. "We've got what we came for. Let's get back to the boat." Reluctantly Furmanov took a last look out into the dark, storm-racked landscape and dragged Mabbitt to his feet. He knew she was right but being denied the opportunity to kill Jordan rankled with him. As they made their way down to their small boat on the sand he scanned the area behind them hoping that Mabbitt's protector would attempt a rescue. No such attempt was made.

Fifteen minutes later Jordan stood at the water's edge and watched the cabin cruiser's lights disappear round the headland, the driving rain pouring down his face. As he stood alone he was gripped by the overwhelming feeling that he had let Mabbitt down. They had been through so much together, for so long, Jordan found it difficult to accept that he would probably never see the man he regarded as his friend again. In the eerie orange glow of the burning fishing boat he thought he saw something small being tossed around in the waves near the beach. He flicked on the torch and shone its beam a few feet ahead of him in the water. A bloodstained green woollen hat had snagged on a rock. Jordan cursed. He took consolation from the thought that Tug had died the fearless soldier he undoubtedly was, once again feeling needed.

Jordan extinguished the light and watched the *Argus* slip angrily below the surface. He had a long way to go and no idea how to get there. Turning up his collar against the elements, he trudged back up the incline towards the cottage. He was sure of one thing. If nothing else he would keep his word to Mabbitt and kill Harry Grant.

CHAPTER FOURTEEN

Michael Prentiss slowly opened his eyes. The bass drum pounding in his head made it difficult for him to focus. Gradually the blurring cleared and he could see a familiar face anxiously looking down at him. "Grace, is that you?" he said weakly. Grace Fisher smiled and told him not to try and move. Aware that he was lying in a large bed, Prentiss lifted his hand and touched his throbbing head. The momentary surprise of feeling the heavy bandaging instantly disappeared as a searing pain racked his chest causing him to gasp in agony.

"I told you not to move," Grace gently rebuked as she took his hand and replaced it under the duvet. The pain began to subside and Prentiss steadied his breathing once more.

"How bad is it?" Prentiss asked, noticing a drip in his arm.

"Well, considering you threw yourself off a speeding train into a canyon in the dark, I'm amazed that you're still alive." The male voice sounded crabby and irascible. Prentiss looked towards the voice in the dimly-lit room. A short, stocky man wearing a plaid suit was standing by the draped windows. Aged in his late fifties, he looked at Prentiss with not inconsiderable disdain. He walked over to the bed and peered down at him, a pair of half-moon spectacles perched precariously on the end of his fat nose. "Leonard Freeman, Grace's doctor and, luckily for you, a close family friend."

"I had to call him, Michael. I thought you were dying," Grace said, pouring a glass of water and holding it to Prentiss' lips. He sipped it slowly.

"In answer to your question, young man," Freeman continued, "you have a fractured skull, three cracked ribs together with multiple contusions and severe bruising." He paused then added, "Oh yes, and a dislocated shoulder, although I popped that back in for you while you were unconscious. You will have a great deal of residual pain from that as it appears to have had a bullet through it at some point."

"Nothing too serious, then?" Prentiss said sarcastically.

"You're a lucky man, Mister Prentiss. Although if you'll accept some advice from an old country doctor, you'll wait until the train gets into the station before you try and get off next time," Freeman said gruffly without raising a smile. For the next few minutes he examined Prentiss concluding that he was happy with his patient's progress. "A couple of weeks bed rest and we'll have you up and about again."

"No, I can't stay here for two weeks. I've got to get going. I have to meet some friends on the Twenty-fourth."

"Then I'm afraid you're going to be late."

"You don't understand, it's vitally important that I get there," Prentiss insisted.

"And I don't think *you* understand, Mister Prentiss. Today is the Twenty-ninth. You have been here for more than a week in and out of consciousness." As Prentiss lay stunned, trying to come to terms with the fact that he had lost nine days, Doctor Freeman left saying that he would call by again tomorrow.

"Leonard's a good friend; he won't say anything," Grace assured him as she returned to the bed and perched on the edge.

"How did you find me?"

"By sheer luck. After you phoned me to say that you were jumping off the train I drove down to Merrimack and searched along the railway track. It took me an hour to find you. When I did, you were in such a mess. You were unconscious and covered in blood. Somehow I managed to get you back here and called Leonard."

"What have you told him about me?"

"Nothing. I didn't say and he didn't ask. Like I said, he's a good friend."

"Thanks, Grace. I'm sorry I had to get you involved."

"Well, now that I am you can tell me what is going on," Grace demanded. "And don't give me any bull about it being top secret, or too dangerous for me to know or some other damn excuse because I don't want to hear it. So just tell me." Prentiss looked at the woman he had met two years earlier. She was no longer the frightened, fragile person he remembered. She was strong now; confident and in control. Prentiss decided to tell her everything. Explaining in detail the sequence of events that led to him jumping from the train, he left nothing out. Grace sat quietly and listened attentively until Prentiss finished. "I remember the name Grant. He was Steve Bannon's man, wasn't he? The one he sent to kill you and your friends for Tom?" She helped him sip some more water. "And now you think he's involved in some kind of political assassination at this summit?"

"It's what he does," Prentiss observed soberly. Grace mulled it over in her mind. She owed Michael Prentiss a great deal. Without his help she would not now be free of her evil late husband, Thomas.

"What do you need me to do?"

"I need to get to Iceland, Grace but I have no passport, no

money and I'm being actively sought by most of the law enforcement agencies of this country."

"There may be a way," she replied after thinking for a moment. "Try and get some rest. I'll see what I can do." She smiled as she got up to leave. "It's funny, I didn't think I would ever see you again. When you left me tied up here that night you were so badly hurt. I wasn't even sure that you were still alive. And now here you are again; still alone fighting the bad guys, still getting hurt."

"To be honest my life isn't usually nearly as exciting as this. I keep being led astray by my friends."

MacIntyre watched Doctor Freeman drive away from the Fisher residence from his concealed observation point opposite the wrought iron front gates. He had been following him for four days now. Every day Freeman had come to the large house west of Concord and remained for many hours. The more he watched, the more MacIntyre was convinced that the good doctor was either having some torrid affair or that he was treating somebody so ill they should be in hospital.

Having returned to the jump point and unable to find Prentiss, the FBI had co-ordinated a grid search lasting two days resulting in nothing. Examination of the assaulted passenger's cell phone records revealed that Prentiss had contacted a payphone at Concord railway station minutes before he jumped. MacIntyre considered the distinct possibility that he had been talking to either Colonel Mabbitt or Richard Jordan. What it did confirm to him was that Prentiss had been forced, rather than intended, to leave the train before it reached his destination of Concord.

With no leads to go on, the FBI had scaled down the search to little more than a police APB to stop and apprehend if seen. This meant that MacIntyre was now working pretty much alone. Sir Neil Peterson's final phone call to him had been both brusque and to the point. Get me results or don't bother coming back. Concluding that Prentiss must certainly have injured himself and would require medical attention, MacIntyre concentrated his search in Concord. After all, that was where Prentiss had been heading to meet whoever was now surely helping him.

Having drawn up a list of doctors in and around Concord, and using the pretence of being new to the area, MacIntyre had found himself chatting to a rather charming middle-aged receptionist in Doctor Freeman's outer office. Doctor Leonard Freeman had a small independent practice in the exclusive south-west area of the city. His surgery was nicely appointed as were his wealthy patients. Offering her most profound apologies she told him that unfortunately the Doctor had rather unexpectedly cancelled all his appointments for the rest of the week and that he would have to come back. That was enough for MacIntyre to start looking into Freeman's movements a little more closely.

MacIntyre had made some discreet enquiries about the person that was occupying so much of Freeman's time. Grace Fisher was a beautiful young woman who lived alone in the large country house a few miles west of Concord. Widowed two years earlier when her husband was murdered during a burglary at their home, she devoted her time and incredible wealth supporting a number of charities and fund-raising foundations.

Just before the electric gates to the Fisher residence closed with a loud clang, MacIntyre slipped through them and walked up the long gravel driveway. Ringing the doorbell he waited between the white stone pillars of the portico. With little more than a combination of assumptions and gut instinct that Prentiss was inside, he decided that he would shake the tree and see what fell out.

Invited inside by a maid, he stood in the hall and waited for Grace Fisher to appear. He only had a few seconds alone before Grace emerged from a room off the landing and skipped down the curved staircase. MacIntyre smiled and produced a small identification card. She looked at it and raised her eyebrows with surprise. "Wow, you're a long way from home Mister MacIntyre," she said brightly, tucking her blonde hair behind her ear. "What can I do for the British Security Services?" MacIntyre showed her a photograph of Prentiss.

"I'm looking for this Englishman. His name is Michael Prentiss but he may be using one of the aliases Callum Daniels or Mario Danetti." MacIntyre watched her face while she looked at the picture. There wasn't a suggestion of either recognition or anxiety in her expression. Grace shook her head and apologised, certain that she hadn't seen anyone like that.

"Is that so?" MacIntyre replied suspiciously, holding her stare. "He may be accompanied by these two men." Producing two more photographs he handed them to Grace. "They're also both British. Charles Mabbitt and Richard Jordan." He tapped each picture as he said their names. Again she shook her head.

"No, I'm afraid I haven't seen them either." She handed back the three photographs. There was an awkward silence as MacIntyre nodded thoughtfully.

"So nobody matching Prentiss' description has been here, possibly injured in some way and needing a doctor?"

"No, sorry," Grace said apologetically, beginning to find the man's intense stare and faint smile unnerving. "I really can't help you, Mister MacIntyre."

"Hmm." MacIntyre narrowed his eyes. "Are you sure about that, Mrs Fisher? I would hate to think that you were lying to me."

"I've told you," Grace said angrily. "I haven't seen this Prentiss, Colonel Mabbitt or the other one, whatever his name was. So if you'll excuse me, I think you had better leave."

"That's very interesting," MacIntyre said coolly as he reached the already open door. "I didn't say that Mabbitt was a Colonel. If you change your mind you can contact me through the Concord Police Department. I'm sure we'll meet again soon." MacIntyre bid her a good afternoon and left, satisfied that the lovely Mrs Fisher was indeed hiding Prentiss.

From a front upper window, Michael Prentiss clutched his chest and watched MacIntyre walk away from the house. He had listened to the conversation in the hallway, recognising the MI5 man's name from Mabbitt and Jordan's encounters with him. "Richard was right," Prentiss thought as MacIntyre turned and looked back at the house as he reached the gates, "you are a cunning little weasel."

"I'm sorry, Michael. He knows you're here." Grace stood in the doorway, annoyed with herself that she could have made such a stupid mistake. Prentiss returned to the bed and told her not to worry.

"It's not your fault, Grace. That guy's a professional. It does complicate things though." He laid back and closed his eyes, his head spinning. As MacIntyre had found his way here believing that Mabbitt and Jordan were with him, Prentiss considered, they were clearly having more luck than he was.

"I have a private plane that can get us to Iceland," Grace announced quietly. "I can make the arrangements and we can leave in the morning." Prentiss opened his eyes.

"What do you mean, we?"

"I'm going with you," she replied indignantly. "Anyway, you won't be allowed on board unless I'm with you. Now, you get some rest and I'll get you something to eat. You need to build your strength up. It's going to be a long journey." Deciding it was pointless to argue, Prentiss closed his eyes again and waited for the pounding in his head to stop.

In a private hanger at Concord airport, Grace's Hawker 800 executive jet had been fuelled and the flight plan to Iceland logged. Despite Doctor Freeman's vehement protestations that Prentiss was in no condition to travel, he had prepared his patient as best he could to make the arduous journey. Tightly bandaging his ribs and giving him powerful painkillers, Freeman had left Prentiss with a stark warning. "I don't know who or what you are, Michael, but Grace trusts you so I'm going to give you some advice. You need to start taking care of yourself, young man. I can only imagine how you got some of the injury scars you have. If you're not careful you're going to take a lot of years off your retirement."

At just after 8am, Grace's Cadillac limousine swept into the hangar where the plane's two man crew were waiting. They looked uncomfortably at each other as Grace and Prentiss got out. Asking the pilot if everything was ready as she walked towards them, Grace sensed that something was wrong.

"Good morning, Mrs Fisher," MacIntyre said appearing in the doorway of the aircraft. "And Mister Prentiss, looking rather the worse for wear. I'm afraid you're permission to take off appears to have been refused." His tone was bright with a hint of mock sympathy. He stood in front of Prentiss and winced as he looked carefully at his bruised face. "Where is Colonel Mabbitt?"

"He's not here. I came to the States on my own."

"Is that so? So why did Mabbitt want an ex-mercenary dead? After all that is what you do for him, isn't it, Michael? Murder people on the quiet? The Colonel uses you for those awkward little unofficial jobs he doesn't want connected with his usual nefarious activities in 'The Det'."

"Are you really that bloody stupid?" Prentiss said exasperatedly. "I'm not here to kill anybody, for Mabbitt or anyone else, come to that. I didn't murder that thug in Washington. I've been set up by the man that did to stop me getting back with what I know." MacIntyre stared intently into Prentiss' eyes.

"You ought to hear what Michael's got to say," Grace said breaking the silence.

"I'm listening," MacIntyre said eventually.

"Colonel Mabbitt discovered an assassination plot at the forthcoming Reagan-Gorbachev arms summit in Reykjavik."

"Who's the target?"

"Don't know. I do know that a senior White House official has supplied detailed plans of the summit to a known assassin by the name of Harry Grant."

"So why hasn't Mabbitt made this official and taken it to the

JIC?"

"No proof. And, from what I understand of Sir Neil Peterson, his hatred for the Colonel would impair what little judgement he has."

"So Mabbitt and Jordan are in Iceland are they? And you're planning to meet up with them and save the day like the three bloody musketeers, I suppose."

"Well, that's really up to you isn't it?" Prentiss replied. MacIntyre frowned.

"I'm not sure I believe any of this," he said warily, "but my job's to find Mabbitt and if he's in Iceland, then you're going to take me to him." He turned to Grace. "Congratulations, Mrs Fisher, your permission to fly to Iceland has just been granted."

CHAPTER FIFTEEN

Mabbitt watched a small black spider scurry out of a crack in the wall close to the ceiling above his head. He shuddered with the combination of a lifelong dislike of anything that crawled and the increasing cold. It was impossible for him to gauge just how long he had been in the small windowless room. In the absence of a blanket or pillow, he lay on his side, pulled his knees up to his chin and folded his arms to keep warm. He looked at the heavy metal door. It wouldn't be long before one of the two blank-faced thugs, he had named 'Pinky and Perky', would come in and silently put a metal plate and mug on the floor and leave.

Having been drugged once aboard the cabin cruiser, he had woken with a blinding headache on the narrow cast iron bed to discover his wristwatch, belt and shoes had been removed. A single unshaded bulb hanging from a worn pendent in the ceiling lit the eight feet by five room. It was cold. The unpainted brick walls and concrete floor offered no warmth and the air was damp and stale. Mabbitt had tried to glean some clue as to his location but there was nothing, not a sound, not a smell that gave him any idea as to where he was.

Two heavy bolts were drawn back and the door opened. 'Perky' came in and placed the daily cheese sandwich and water on the floor. This was the sixth time he had been brought the same meagre offering. Mabbitt sighed. Six cheeses sandwiches, six days of incarceration. "I suppose a fillet steak washed down with bottle of Saint Emilion is out of the question?" Mabbitt asked hopefully as the door slammed shut and the bolts were slid across. "Hmm, thought so."

As he ate the last of the disgusting sandwich the bolts were drawn back and the door opened again. This was the first deviation to the routine since he had woken up in his cell six days earlier so Mabbitt was intrigued as to what was about to come. He didn't recognise the tall, well dressed man smiling warmly at him from the doorway. "Colonel Mabbitt, Charles. May I call you Charles?" Koskov said in his long Texan drawl as he entered rubbing his hands together in the cold air.

"And who might you be?" Mabbitt asked politely, sipping the water.

"Kowalski's the name, Mickey Kowalski." He extended his hand but Mabbitt ignored it.

"Where am I?"

"Somewhere safe." Koskov withdrew his hand but maintained his toothy smile. "I know what you must be thinking. Why have I been brought to such a terrible place? The truth is, somebody is doing a little job for me and he won't do it unless I give you to him."

"Harry Grant," Mabbitt said dispassionately, tossing his plate onto the mattress next to him.

"Charles," Koskov said wagging his finger in astonishment. "Harry said you were one smart cookie but that's impressive. Yes, you are quite right. I'm afraid Harry has taken a real dislike to you, blames you for the death of his girlfriend. So sad; a lovely girl," he said with a melancholic tone. "When she died it just about tipped him over the edge and you know Harry, he was one crazy mixed up psycho to begin with."

"Yes," Mabbitt said thoughtfully. "Tell me, Mister Kowalski, this little job he's doing. Does he know that he is in fact working for the KGB? You are KGB, aren't you?" Koskov let out a loud laugh.

"Hell no! He thinks he's doing it for the good old U, S of A. I think it's better that way, don't you? And don't go getting any crazy notion that you're going to tell him how you've put all the pieces together. Harry doesn't get his hands on you until he's done the job. I don't want him to get the right idea about me." Koskov turned to the door. "Camera!" Within seconds 'Perky' came in and handed him a Polaroid camera. "Smile," Koskov said as he took a photograph of Mabbitt. "Just something to prove to Harry that I've got you safely tucked away." He pulled the picture from the front of the camera and watched it develop.

"Why would you risk war between Russia and America? Surely you must see that such an outcome is inevitable?"

"Inevitable? I don't think so. There will be no retaliation from either side if both leaders are killed and the assassin doesn't survive to be questioned."

"Thus concealing the true identity of the target," Mabbitt concluded. "That's very clever. By the by, just as a matter of interest, who is the target?" Koskov didn't reply. He just smiled knowingly at Mabbitt.

"I'm afraid I really must be going, Charles. I've a long and rather tedious flight ahead of me." Koskov turned to leave then added coldly, "Please don't get any cute ideas about trying to escape. It's very difficult to run when both your legs are broken."

Two days later Koskov got off the boat that brought him from the mainland to Ko Similan. He was weary and felt as if he was permanently jet-lagged with constant travelling. As he walked along the wooden quay in the midday heat, he decided that when this operation was over he would have earned himself a long, relaxing vacation. As a self-employed engineering consultant based in Washington DC, nobody questioned why he made his many journeys overseas. Which was, of course, why it was chosen as his cover in the United States.

Grant watched the American in the white panama hat get out of the twenty year old Jeep that served as the taxi service on the island. He studied him suspiciously from the veranda of his house with his dark brown eyes. Koskov greeted him with his now customary slap on the back and exuberant grin. After the ubiquitous enquiries about the journey, Grant wasted no time in asking if Mabbitt had been captured. The callous excitement became more and more visible in his eyes as Koskov handed him the photograph. Grant stared at it, studying every aspect of the man's face.

"Where is he?" Grant said finally.

"On ice somewhere uncomfortable. You can have him when the job's done." Koskov's tone was unequivocal. Grant raised an eyebrow but didn't voice his obvious frustration. "How are your preparations progressing?"

"Okay." He tossed the photograph onto the table. "In fact I'm glad you're here. I have something you might be interested in seeing."

Grant led Koskov a quarter of a mile into the island to a large clearing. A small bamboo hut stood in the centre, both the door and single shuttered window wide open. As they drew closer, Koskov could just make out, as he peered through the doorway, an elderly man tied to a chair, his mouth taped shut.

"Who's this?" Koskov said as he and Grant stood inside the hut. Grant was expressionless as he looked down at the terrified man.

"Nobody," he replied simply. The old man flinched and cried out in pain as Grant leant forward and pulled up his blood stained khaki cotton shirt. Koskov saw a bleeding five inch gash in the man's stomach crudely held together with eight large stitches.

"How long has it been in there?" Koskov asked looking at the clearly infected wound.

"Twenty-four hours. Of course, this is just a test subject. The actual implant will be conducted by a surgeon in a sterile environment. No risk of infection."

"Good." Koskov nodded. He and Grant left the sweltering heat of the hut and walked to the edge of the clearing. They stood amongst the trees two hundred yards from the isolated bamboo shack. Grant took a small black plastic box from his pocket and extended the six inch telescopic aerial at the top.

"Remote control detonator," Grant said. "The device has a built-in timer, this activates it." He pressed one of the two buttons on the unit, illuminating a small red light. "I'll be using a sixty minute delay for the operation but, for demonstration purposes, this one is set for one second." Koskov smiled approvingly. "This is the part I really like," Grant said, grinning. The two men watched the elderly rice farmer struggling to free himself as Grant pressed the second button. Almost instantly the farmer and the hut disintegrated in a huge, deafening explosion. Koskov looked at Grant who was as wide-eyed and excited as a schoolboy watching his first firework display. "That was using just half the amount of the explosive," Grant explained, pushing the aerial back in with the palm of his hand.

"Good work, Harry. You've done a great job. How long before I can make the arrangements for the package to be inserted into the carrier?"

"I need to make a few adjustments but everything should ready within the next seventy-two hours. Any problems your end?" Koskov hesitated at Grant's question then replied.

"There may be a possible containment issue. A young British guy calling himself Callum Daniels was questioning Griffin in Washington about meeting Roisin in Belfast."

"What did Griffin tell him?" Grant asked watching the smoke plume up into the clear blue sky.

"He spilled all he knew. Daniels managed to escape before I could neutralise him but fortunately he was believed to have been killed when he later jumped from a train running from the police." Grant looked at Koskov, all trace of his former smile gone.

"This Daniels, describe him to me." Koskov described in detail the man he had forced at gunpoint to the car park at Dulles airport.

"That's Michael Prentiss, one of Mabbitt's killers. If they didn't find a body then trust me, he's still alive. He leads a charmed life that one," Grant said venomously. "Find him, Mickey. If Mabbitt sent him to talk to Griffin then he may have worked out what we're doing."

"Mabbitt can't do any harm to the operation now."

"If Prentiss is involved, Jordan won't be far away."

"Who?"

"Richard Jordan, one of Mabbitt's secret soldiers and he's good, very good. When you had Mabbitt picked up was there anyone with him?" Koskov looked intently into Grant's searching eyes. From Furmanov's report to General Durov, this man, Jordan sounded exactly like Mabbitt's bodyguard who had caused so many problems during the kidnap operation.

"No," he said assuredly. Telling lies had been Koskov's stock-in-trade for so long there was no suggestion from his expression that he wasn't telling anything other than the truth. Grant nodded slowly.

"I'll bring the package to you in a few days. In the mean time, you find Prentiss and you kill him."

It was 10pm by the time Koskov had returned to his now familiar Phuket hotel to make a telephone call to General Durov. During the long journey, he had considered the implications of what Grant had told him about Mabbitt's men. As he thought about the young man he now knew to be Michael Prentiss, he began to feel uneasy. If, as Grant suspected, he was still alive he posed a significant threat to the operation. There was something dangerous about Prentiss. He was certainly resourceful, that was clear, but it was more than that. When he had looked into his eyes he had seen no fear. Having listened to the recording of his interrogation of Griffin, Koskov concluded that Prentiss would do whatever was necessary to get results and that was what made him dangerous.

"What is it you need this time, Mikhail Alexandreivich?" General Durov asked gruffly.

"There are two things, Comrade General. First I want you to raise tension between the Soviet Union and the Americans."

"And why would I want to do that?"

"The relationship between Gorbachev and Reagan is too

amicable at present. I want to introduce an element of instability before the summit. It is important that the atmosphere is one of suspicion and distrust between the two leaders."

"If they are both to die why should we bother with such a tactic?"

"Let's just call it a fall-back position in the unlikely event that anything were to go wrong with the operation." Durov remained silent so Koskov continued. "Earlier today the Americans arrested General Zakharov from the Soviet UN Mission. I want you to have one of the American journalists in Moscow arrested for espionage in retaliation."

"Who?"

"Who is irrelevant. Just ensure that he is innocent." There was a long pause from Durov.

"I will arrange for it to be done. You said there were two things."

"Yes. I believe that Colonel Mabbitt may have two of his men on their way to Iceland to stop us achieving our goal. I need them located urgently."

"How have you allowed this to happen, Major?" Durov growled angrily. "You gave me your assurance that the total secrecy for this operation remained completely intact."

"It appears that Colonel Mabbitt is far more shrewd than we anticipated. And, with respect, Comrade General," Koskov said controlling his rising temper, "if I hadn't had him abducted this issue would never have come to light." There was a tense silence between the two men.

"Very well, Major Koskov. Give me the details of these two men and I will have them dealt with. But understand this, there are to be no more security breaches. It would be a great pity if the operation and all those involved in it had to be, erased." Durov chose his last word carefully to leave no doubt in Koskov's mind what would happen to him.

"Understood." Koskov spat out the word.

"What are the names of these two men?"

"Richard Jordan, he's the retired operator from Mabbitt's unit that Furmanov encountered."

"And the other?"

"Michael Prentiss. He's something of an enigma but seems to be used for special covert operations."

"When these two have been located, are they to be detained with Mabbitt?" Koskov thought about Durov's question for a moment.

"No, eliminate them both."

CHAPTER SIXTEEN

Richard Jordan leant against the rail of the Icelandic trawler as it entered Reykjavik harbour. He sniffed his jacket sleeve and grimaced at the fetid stench of fish. It had been a long and difficult journey but at last he was finally in Iceland. He looked at the day and date on his watch and swore under his breath, Monday 1st September. If everything had gone according to plan in Washington, Michael would have already been here for more than a week. Still, he thought, better that than having to overcome the endless obstacles that had beset his journey during the last few days.

As he reflected on all that had happened and what was still to come, Jordan's thoughts turned to Colonel Mabbitt. It had been nine days since he had spent a cold night in the crofter's cottage having watched the cabin cruiser disappear with Mabbitt on board. Deciding it was pointless trying to stumble around in the dark, he had woken as it began to get light only to discover that it was raining again. Cursing loudly as he pulled the collar of his green wax jacket up around his ears, he threw his bag over his shoulder and set out. Having examined the map before leaving the *Argus*, he knew that he was in the largely unpopulated far south west of the island. He had headed due west, the stunning beauty of South Uist completely lost on him as he trudged over the sodden grassland in the pouring rain.

Following a chance lift a couple of hours later from a farmer driving north on the only 'B' road for miles around, Jordan had found himself in the small town of Lochboisdale. Being little more than a ferry terminal with a few amenities for the local population, he spent most of the morning avoiding the increasing interest of the inquisitive resident police constable.

Personal Retributions

It was while getting a hot meal in the Lochboisdale Hotel and considering how on earth he was going to get to Iceland that he found the answer to his transport problem. Moira Keating-Sinclair was one of those intimidating school ma'am types with curly grey hair, a ruddy complexion on her large moon-face and a personality that could only be described as direct. On holiday alone, sailing round the islands of Western Scotland in her twenty-six foot sloop, she offered to take Jordan as far as the Isle of Lewis. He had gratefully accepted and by late that same evening was standing on the docks in Stornoway. Offering to work his passage to Iceland, following a few drinks with some of the crew of the Icelandic trawler in the pub later that night, Jordan spent the next week gutting and packing fish into huge crates aboard the *Sjómaður*. Finally, the trawler docked at Reykjavik and he slipped quietly ashore before the port authorities started asking awkward questions.

Jordan shivered. At just after nine in the morning it was barely six degrees and the icy Arctic wind made it feel colder still. He walked past the gleaming white building of the *Hotel Borg* on the opposite side of the street to make sure it wasn't being watched. Located on *Pósthússtræti* close to Reykjavik cathedral, the hotel was the agreed rendezvous for him and Mabbitt to meet Prentiss. Ten minutes later, after another walk-past and certain that the hotel wasn't under surveillance from the outside, he went in.

Taking the stairs to the second floor, Jordan took a Browning automatic from the bag, screwed on the silencer and tucked it into his waistband. Confirming that Mister Callum Daniels was staying in room 204, the blonde receptionist had added that his friends, a man and a woman, were in 202 and 206. Something had gone wrong. He knew that Prentiss should be alone and had a horrible feeling that he was being held by the same two Russians that had grabbed Mabbitt. If that was the case, from what he'd seen of them, overpowering them wasn't going to be easy.

Jordan emerged from the stairwell. The corridor was deserted. Hiding his bag beneath a small table against the wall, he began to move cautiously down the hallway. Reaching room 202, he listened momentarily outside the door. There was no sound from inside. Drawing his gun he continued on to 204 and listened again. Still nothing. Jordan let out a long, slow breath and knocked on the door. "Package for Mister Daniels." He cringed at his attempt at an Icelandic accent. There was movement inside then the door opened. Prentiss stood in the doorway, his face remaining blank as he recognised the man in front of him.

"Yes?" Prentiss said looking down as Jordan produced his gun. Jordan looked at him intently as Prentiss flicked his eyes towards the open door. That was all Jordan needed. Shoulder-charging the door, he felt somebody against the other side of it held against the wall. He slammed it again hard then swung the door shut revealing MacIntyre slumped on the floor unconscious, blood pouring from his nose.

"MacIntyre?" Jordan said relieving him of his gun. "What's he doing here?" He handed the weapon to Prentiss.

"Long story. Where the bloody hell have you been, and what is that smell?"

"I came the scenic route. Who's this?" Jordan asked looking over Prentiss' shoulder at the attractive blonde woman standing silently in the corner of the room.

"This is Grace Fisher. She's a friend."

"The lawyer's widow?"

"You'll have to forgive my friend, Grace," Prentiss said as he introduced her to Jordan. "He normally lives alone with only sheep for company."

"What happened to you?" Jordan said looking closely at Prentiss' face.

"I fell off a train," Prentiss replied irritably then suddenly realised that Jordan was on his own. "Where's the Colonel?" Jordan ran his hand wearily through his hair.

"That's where it gets complicated," he sighed. "Help me get this monkey tied up and we can tell each other our tales of woe."

"Okay, but you will have a bath first, won't you?"

Two hours later Jordan had showered, shaved and was dressed in the new clothes Grace had bought for him from a Reykjavik department store. MacIntyre sat uncomfortably in an armchair, his hands bound tightly behind his back. He had listened as Jordan and Prentiss had in turn recounted the events that had led each of them to that point.

"So what do we do now?" Prentiss said. "And how are we going to get the Colonel back?"

"Back from where?" Jordan said with angry frustration. "We don't even know where he is. In fact, we don't know very much at all." They both fell silent. MacIntyre stifled a laugh and shook his head as he looked at the two men in front of him. "What?" Jordan said savagely.

"You boys have got no idea what you're doing, have you?"

"Why don't you just be quiet?" Prentiss said.

"Look, I can help you," he said authoritatively. "It's clear to me from what you've both said that it's all connected." Prentiss and Jordan looked at each other then reluctantly Jordan allowed MacIntyre to continue. "During a routine surveillance operation, Mabbitt discovers a link between the target, Roisin O'Sullivan and Harry Grant, the man that murdered his wife two years ago. So Mabbitt, being the tenacious old sod that he is, does some digging around on his own trying to locate Grant. While doing this he stumbles across a possible assassination plot at the arms summit next month. The fact that Griffin told you, Michael, that he was blackmailed by O'Sullivan to provide information about the summit does give such a plot some credence."

"To kill Reagan," Prentiss added.

"Possibly, but we don't know that for certain."

"But the KGB?" Jordan queried. "Mabbitt was certain that the two that snatched him were KGB."

"Oh undoubtedly they were. What you have to remember is that you two deal with terrorists whereas I catch spies. The difference is that terrorists, although devious and sometimes very cunning, are fundamentally just murderers. Spies on the other hand are professionals. They use deceit, misdirection and deflection to operate successfully. It's all smoke and mirrors. I am certain that we're dealing with a soviet clandestine operation either officially sanctioned or orchestrated by rogue elements of the Politburo. What scares me is the possibility that Reagan isn't the target."

"You think the Russians are planning to kill Gorbachev?"

"That can't be ruled out."

Personal Retributions

"I can't believe that Grant would work for the Russians," Jordan said shaking his head. "I know how he thinks, the way he works. He may not be sane but he is a patriot, I'm sure of that."

"He probably doesn't know they're Russian. You're forgetting Michael's friend at Dulles airport."

"But he was American," Jordan protested.

"They don't all wear Cossack hats and go round singing '*Kalinka*' you know," MacIntyre said sarcastically. "No, he was KGB alright, had to be. Like I said, smoke and mirrors."

"We need to find him," Prentiss said quietly.

"And what about the Colonel?" Jordan added.

"One thing at a time. Chances are Mabbitt is still alive. If they wanted him dead they would have killed him rather than going to all the trouble of kidnapping him." MacIntyre thought for a moment then looked at Prentiss. "Your American at the airport sounds like the helpful bystander who reported seeing you murder that thug. So that's where we start." Prentiss looked at a sceptical Jordan and nodded.

"Okay," Prentiss agreed. "You contact your friends in the FBI and see what you can find out about this guy. Richard and I are going to have a little look at the summit venue."

"There's one more thing," MacIntyre said irritably. "Now that we're all on the same side, how about untying my bloody hands?"

Höfði was a large white detached house standing remote and alone with its back to the sea at Félagstun, close to Reykjavik airport. Jordan and Prentiss stood at the lawned grounds' perimeter fence and studied the location of the forthcoming summit. They speculated how Grant planned to successfully eliminate the target and then, more importantly, manage to escape.

"I can't see how he's going to do it," Jordan admitted finally, staring at the building. He noticed Prentiss holding his ribs. "I'm sorry I got you involved, Michael."

"Don't be," Prentiss replied "I'm not."

"You did well in Washington. It couldn't have been easy, getting Griffin to talk I mean."

"Do you know what, Richard?" Prentiss said distantly. "It really wasn't hard at all."

MacIntyre hung up the phone and grinned triumphantly at Grace. His call to the FBI in Washington DC had lasted fifteen minutes and the information he had requested was being faxed to the hotel reception downstairs at that moment. "Is it the same man that tried to kidnap Michael?" Grace asked.

"It sounds very much like him. There's a photo in the stuff they're faxing through. Michael will be able to identify him from that. I'll pop down to reception and get it." MacIntyre opened the door and stepped out of the room. It was a casual glance down the hallway at the man and woman getting out of the elevator that made him feel uneasy. He looked again. There was definitely something about them, something familiar. MacIntyre searched his memory as they began to walk towards him. It took a couple of seconds then he remembered. He burst back inside the hotel room and locked the door.

What is it?" Grace said as she watched MacIntyre search the room. "MacIntyre, you're scaring me."

"Do you know where Jordan has hidden the weapons?"

"Weapons? No. Why do you need weapons?" Her voice was getting increasingly anxious as she followed him through the connecting door into the adjoining hotel room.

"Because the two Russians that kidnapped Mabbitt have just got out of the elevator," MacIntyre said, his face pale with fear. He knew they were in trouble having seen first hand what they were capable of when they had killed Jones in Cornwall. He closed the connecting door and locked it. As he did so the door to the next room was kicked open with a splintering crash. MacIntyre grabbed Grace's arm and, putting his finger to his lips for her to keep quiet, pulled her away from the door. They could hear the next room being searched. It was only a matter of time before the two KGB agents came through the connecting door.

"We've got to get the fax from reception and warn Jordan and Prentiss," MacIntyre whispered. Grace nodded, her eyes growing wider and wider as she heard movement from the other side of the connecting door. Taking her hand, MacIntyre quietly led Grace into the hallway. They ran towards the elevator. MacIntyre jabbed at the 'down' button. The elevator car began its agonisingly slow ascent from the ground floor. As MacIntyre continued to press the button Eva Nedelyayev appeared in the hallway and called to Furmanov. MacIntyre pushed Grace through the stairwell door. "Run, Grace!" he yelled, then turned and sprinted up the corridor towards Eva.

Breathing hard, Grace dashed down the stairs not daring to look back. Stumbling into the foyer, she ran to the desk and asked for the fax. Nervously she looked behind her as she waited for the receptionist to bring it. Snatching it out of her hand, Grace ran for the double doors of the hotel entrance and out into the street. Frantically she looked for a cab. Seconds later the doors to the hotel behind her burst open and Eva and Furmanov ran down the steps. Without hesitating, Grace sprinted across *Pósthússtræti* and onto the open grassy area opposite. The Russian agents gave chase to the sound of screeching tyres and honking car horns.

With her heart pounding in her chest, Grace turned left and ran towards the cathedral. The cold air stung her throat as she panted, running faster than she had ever done before.

"That's Grace," Prentiss said beginning to quicken his pace. He and Jordan had walked the half mile from *Höfði* and had reached Parliament House when he saw her. "What's she running from?"

"Them," Jordan said pointing to Eva and Furmanov who were gaining on her with almost every stride. Prentiss called out to her but with the noise of the traffic she was too far away to hear. In a blind panic, she ran across *Kirkjustræti* and into the cathedral. Jordan and Prentiss began to run but Prentiss soon fell behind, gripping his side and fighting for breath. Jordan looked back and began to slow down but Prentiss waved him on and angrily shouted for him to go.

Jordan reached the cathedral entrance thirty seconds after he had watched Eva and Furmanov run inside. He drew his gun and went in. The air was still and silent. The tall, long, narrow windows, high in the walls, cast strips of bright sunlight on the floor. Jordan screwed on the silencer as he moved slowly down the cathedral, remaining close to the wall. The building was empty except for an elderly woman with a mop and bucket judiciously cleaning the floor.

Grace had run to the end of the majestically cavernous building, up the half dozen steps and hidden behind the altar table. She crouched there, still clutching the fax, not daring to move. Furmanov and Eva had split up and were making their way up the cathedral on opposite walls concealed by the towering grey-white pillars. Slowly, silently they moved towards the altar. Jordan caught a glimpse of Eva a few yards ahead of him and raised his gun. Sensing someone was behind her she darted behind a pillar. Appearing for a second, she fired at Jordan. The bullet from the silenced Makarov pinged off the pillar as he took cover. Furmanov looked across at Eva. She signalled to him to continue up to the altar. She fired again forcing Jordan to remain behind the pillar.

Furmanov reached the light coloured wooden pulpit to the right of the altar. He crouched behind it. From his position Jordan could just about see him but was unable to get a clear shot as Eva had got him pinned down. He tried for a shot but Eva's Makarov coughed again, this time narrowly missing his head. He swore under his breath. Furmanov had worked his way up to the altar table. He smiled sadistically as he saw Grace crouching behind it. Like a prowling cat he delighted in slowly walking round the altar table and standing over her. He raised his gun and levelled it at her head. Grace stared up at him and waited for him to fire. A loud gunshot reverberated around the cathedral. Furmanov's head was suddenly jerked back as the bullet ripped into it just above his left ear. Grace looked over the table and saw Prentiss at the other end of the aisle, his gun still pointing at the altar.

Jordan saw Prentiss and made his move. Breaking cover, he fired repeatedly as he sprinted towards Eva. One of the rounds clipped her shoulder sending her reeling backwards to the ground. Kicking the Makarov out of her reach, Jordan held her at gunpoint.

Grace ran over to Prentiss and threw her arms around him. They stood holding each other for a moment without speaking.

"Where's MacIntyre?" He whispered.

"I think they killed him at the hotel. He stayed so that I could get away with this." She handed him the fax. Prentiss looked at the photograph.

"That's him," Prentiss said quietly. "What do you want to do with her?" Prentiss said as he and Grace walked over to Jordan and looked down at Eva. Jordan smiled.

"Well, firstly we're going to get her out of here before the local plods turn up."

"And then?"

"I'm going to make her tell us where Mabbitt is," Jordan said earnestly. "And then we're going to get him back."

CHAPTER SEVENTEEN

Richard Jordan drove the Honda Civic estate west through the Reykjavik suburbs and out of the city. He had hi-jacked the vehicle at gunpoint as it pulled up outside the cathedral, pulling the driver out onto the pavement as Prentiss had bundled Eva into the back seat behind Grace. Having managed to get clear just minutes before the police arrived, Jordan sped along Route 1, *Suðurlandsvegur*, heading towards *Hveragerði*. It wasn't long before all signs of civilisation disappeared and were replaced by the bleak and unforgiving landscape of Iceland's volcanic interior.

"You don't really expect to make me talk, do you?" Eva said, slumped against the door clutching her shoulder. "I am a professional." Jordan looked at her in the rear view mirror.

"I've interrogated professionals before. They all talked. I don't see any reason to think you'll be any different." His voice was threatening and monotone and his stare, intense.

"What's Mabbitt got to do with the arms summit operation?" Prentiss said. Eva looked at him quizzically.

"I don't know what you're talking about."

"Oh, come on, sweetheart," Jordan said irritably. "It's no coincidence that you lifted Mabbitt just as he discovered an assassination plot at the forthcoming talks being held here next month."

"I know of no such operation," she sneered. Jordan swore, threw the car down a narrow deserted track and skidded to a stop.

"So why go to so much trouble to kidnap Mabbitt?" Jordan asked, turning in his seat to face her. Eva looked at him indignantly.

"Orders."

"And now you've got orders to kill all of us, why?" Prentiss demanded.

"No, just you and him. I don't know who she is." She flashed her eyes at Grace.

"What did you do to MacIntyre, the man that was with me?" Grace feared she already knew the answer but hoped she was wrong.

"He was an irrelevant obstacle and was dealt with accordingly." There was such disdain in her voice and she spoke so matter-of-factly, tears of anger began to well up in Grace's eyes.

"What kind of a monster are you?" Eva responded to her question with a cruel smile. Jordan told Grace to stay in the car as he got out, pulled Eva from the back seat and dragged her to the back of the vehicle. He looked at the bullet wound in her shoulder and grimaced.

"The bullet is still in there. That must really hurt." he said sympathetically then slowly he pushed his thumb into the hole." Eva screamed and writhed in agony.

"*Po' shyol 'na hui!*" she yelled defiantly.

"Just one question, where is Colonel Mabbitt?" He lifted his thumb. "Well?" Eva spat in his face. "Wrong answer." Jordan pressed again. Inside the car they could clearly hear Eva's screams.

"What's he doing to her?" Grace shuffled uncomfortably.

"He's doing what needs to be done," Prentiss replied distantly.

"Where's Mabbitt?" Jordan asked again as he eased off the wound now pouring with thick, red blood. Eva wearily shook her head. He took out his gun and held it to Eva's other shoulder. "Listen to me, love," Jordan hissed. "I can do this all bloody day if I have to. You tell me where Mabbitt is or I'll start again with a nice new bullet hole."

Grace suddenly jumped, startled as she heard a gunshot and then more screaming. "Aren't you going to stop him?"

"Stop him?" Prentiss replied incredulously. "If I thought he needed it I'd go out there and help him." Grace couldn't find the words to reply. She was suddenly overwhelmed, saddened that such a young man could be so damaged.

The door opened and Jordan got back into the car and started the engine. He looked at his blood stained hands on the steering wheel and wiped them as best he could on his trousers. "Well?" Prentiss asked.

"Mabbitt's here in Iceland; about twenty miles away in a deserted farmhouse a mile or so north-east of a place called *Arborg*." Jordan was focused, determined.

"And the woman?"

"No longer a problem."

It was dark by the time Jordan turned off Route 1 and onto the unsurfaced country road beyond *Arborg*. Essentially little more than a track, the road cut a swathe through miles and miles of desolate landscape. Nobody had spoken during the forty minute journey as they each considered what was about to happen. Having to torture Eva weighed heavily on Jordan. It was an element of his former life he was glad to leave behind. Any feelings of guilt for what he had just done were outweighed by the sense of failure he had for allowing Mabbitt to be captured.

Prentiss too was brooding over his actions in killing Furmanov in the cathedral. He felt no remorse, no guilt, in fact, he felt nothing at all. There had been no hesitation when, breathless and in pain, he had finally reached the cathedral. He had acted instinctively just as he had when he had killed before. This time however it was different. This time it was, he searched his feelings until the stark realisation hit him, this time it was easy.

"That must be it," Jordan said, stopping the car and extinguishing the lights. A quarter of a mile away at the end of an even narrower track, a large dilapidated white farmhouse stood alone amidst the flat, bleak landscape. A single light shone dimly in a downstairs room.

"How many?" Prentiss asked pulling the slide back on his Browning automatic.

"Two, maybe," Jordan replied. Telling Grace to stay in the car, he and Prentiss got out and began to walk towards the house. The temperature was tumbling rapidly as an icy wind blew relentlessly from the north. Ignoring the cold, they reached the gable end wall of the farmhouse then made their way round to the lit window. Crouching beneath it, pressed against the wall, Jordan screwed the silencer onto his gun. Slowly he peered through the filthy cracked glass of the undraped window.

"Richard," Prentiss whispered.

"What?"

"You have you got a plan, haven't you?" Jordan crouched down again until his face was only inches away from Prentiss'.

"Yes," he replied assuredly. Prentiss waited a moment for him to elaborate.

"Are you going to tell me what it is?"

"We're going to go in there, kill anyone that tries to kill us, find the Colonel and then run. You go round the back and try and find another way inside."

"What are you going to do?"

"What they least expect," Jordan said smiling. "I'm going to knock on the front door."

Jordan gave Prentiss a few seconds then took a deep breath and banged on the door. He waited with no response. He banged again for longer this time. Seconds later he heard movement from inside. As a heavy bolt was drawn back, he tensed. The door hadn't even opened an inch when Jordan fired two muffled shots through the wood and burst inside. Putting two more rounds into the man now lying on the hallway floor, he stepped over him without pausing and continued into the house.

At the back, Prentiss had unsuccessfully attempted to open the door, held securely by two large bolts. He cursed angrily before smashing a window using the butt of his gun and climbing inside. The unlit room in which he found himself was empty and unused. He crossed to the door. With no idea where in the house Jordan was or exactly how many they were up against, he hesitated before opening the door. No sooner had he done so than the deafening rat-a-tat of sub machine gun fire forced him back into the room. A dozen bullets ripped into the door frame and surrounding wall, splintering the rotting wood. The second Russian stood hunched at the bottom of a staircase off the hallway in the centre of the house. Silently, Jordan emerged from a room behind him. He triggered three rapid shots, the last of which thudded into the man's shoulder. The Russian spun round and fired, stepping into the hallway. As Jordan cried out and fell to the floor, Prentiss broke cover and put five rounds into the man's back.

"Bollocks!" Jordan yelled clutching his calf, furious that he had allowed himself to get shot. Pulling a woollen scarf from the dead man's neck, Prentiss tied it around Jordan's lower leg.

"You're lucky," Prentiss observed. "It's gone straight through. Missed the bone and the artery."

"I must keep reminding myself just how lucky I am," Jordan said with a mixture of irony and sarcasm. A faint but constant banging stopped Prentiss from replying. Helping Jordan to his feet, they followed the sound through a door and down a flight of concrete steps to a basement. Limping heavily, Jordan followed Prentiss through the basement and watched while he unbolted the door at far end.

"Michael, my dear boy!" Mabbitt said triumphantly as Prentiss opened the door. "Would it be terribly ungracious of me to say, about time too?" Although he looked tired, unshaven and dishevelled, his eyes still had their familiar twinkle. Jordan appeared in the doorway. Mabbitt looked at the two injured men and could only imagine what they gone through to get there.

"Let's go, Colonel," Prentiss said, managing a relieved smile. With Jordan helped on either side by Prentiss and Mabbitt, they climbed the steps out of the basement. "I'll go and get the car," Prentiss said as they reached the front door. Opening it, they were dazzled by a semi circle of bright car headlights all switched on simultaneously. The sound of automatic weapons being cocked by the dozen or so men behind the cars' open doors was unmistakable.

"*Sérsveit Ríkislögreglustjórans!* Armed police!" yelled a voice out of the darkness behind the glare of the lights. Jordan swore quietly.

They had no option but to surrender. As Mabbitt looked at all the police firepower in front of them, he sighed heavily.

"Would I be right in thinking that you two have been upsetting the authorities again?"

Yfirlögreglupjónn Lars Sigmusson was the most senior detective in the Icelandic Police Force. Invited as a keynote speaker to the Scandinavian Police Symposium in Helsinki, he had received a telephone call of such gravity he had no alternative than to offer his apologies and return to Reykjavik. Mabbitt, Jordan, Prentiss and Grace had all been held incommunicado at police headquarters until Sigmusson's arrival. Detained in isolation for thirty-six hours, they had all remained silent and resolutely uncooperative.

It was 8am on Thursday 4th September when they were all brought from their cells to a large interview room. Although he was still limping, Jordan's gunshot wound to his leg had been treated and the pain had significantly reduced to little more than a constant ache. The four of them sat together in silence on one side of a metal table. The door opened and a tall, smartly dressed man, close to retirement age, strode in and sat down opposite them. Detective Chief Superintendent Sigmusson placed a file on the table and opening it, read aloud the first page. "One Caucasian male shot dead at the Hotel Borg, believed to be a British Intelligence Officer. Two Soviet nationals, one male, one female, shot dead, both holding diplomatic credentials. Two Caucasian males shot dead at a farmhouse near *Arborg*, identities unknown. The theft, at gunpoint, of a yellow 1985 Honda Civic estate from outside Reykjavik cathedral." Closing the file he interlaced his fingers and rested them on top of it. He looked at each one of the four faces in turn. "So," he asked brightly, "who would like to begin?"

Mabbitt decided that he would speak. "My name is Colonel Charles Mabbitt and I am the commanding officer of the Fourteenth Intelligence Company of Her Majesty's army. I was kidnapped by the now deceased Soviet man and woman and held in what were, quite frankly, dreadful conditions in the farmhouse by the also now deceased two unidentified men." He paused for a moment. "Is there any possibility we might have some tea?" Sigmusson allowed a smile to briefly appear at the corners of his mouth. Mabbitt continued. "These two men very kindly released me from my interminable incarceration. I'm afraid I'm not sure of the young lady's involvement as we have yet to be introduced."

"I see," Sigmusson said, nodding slowly. "Would you care to explain why, with the exception of Mrs Fisher, you and your two good Samaritans here don't appear to have any form of identification and indeed, why there is no official record of the three of you entering Iceland?" Mabbitt thought for a moment.

"No, not really." Anything further Mabbitt was about to say was interrupted by the door opening and a uniformed officer entering with a folded piece of paper. He handed it to Sigmusson and waited at attention for a response.

"He's here?" Sigmusson asked having read the note. The officer nodded. "Have him shown in." Dutifully the policeman left. "Well, Colonel," Sigmusson said leaning forward towards him. "If you aren't prepared to answer my questions then perhaps your visitor will be able to shed some light on the matter."

"Visitor?" Mabbitt furrowed his brow. Having no idea who the mysterious visitor was, he was more than a little intrigued to find out who was about to walk through the door. Prentiss and Jordan looked at each other uneasily. They both had the feeling that whoever it was wasn't going to be leaping to their assistance. The door opened. Mabbitt's eyes narrowed as Sir Neil Peterson swept in and stood beside the seated Sigmusson, a smug, self-satisfied expression on his face. He looked down his nose at Mabbitt triumphantly.

"Hello, Charles."

CHAPTER EIGHTEEN

Gino's was one of Washington DC's more exclusive restaurants with its prominent location on leafy Pennsylvania Avenue. Described in the *Washington Post* as "a sublime dining experience," it was *the* place to be seen in amongst the US capital's rich and famous.

It was almost 11pm when Samuel Griffin and his wife, Samantha, left the restaurant and walked arm in arm down Pennsylvania Avenue. It was a warm, balmy evening and Griffin had taken Samantha to *Gino's* to celebrate their wedding anniversary. In truth, it was Samantha that had booked the table and informed him a week earlier that they were going out to dinner and that his presence was required. They had been married for twelve years, the last four of which she had become more and more disinterested in the man she had met at a White House party. Now, almost completely absorbed by her work as head of cardio-thoracic surgery at the George Washington University Hospital, it suited her to remain with a man that made almost no demands upon her, physically or emotionally.

Samantha decided that she had walked far enough and told Griffin to hail a cab. Obediently he waved at a yellow cab which immediately swerved to the edge of the sidewalk and stopped. He dutifully held the door open as Samantha got in and slid over. As he was about to do the same, Griffin was pushed against the trunk of the cab, a razor sharp stiletto knife held to his throat. "Give me your wallet," the attacker hissed, the hood of his jogging sweatshirt covering his face. Griffin fumbled in his dinner jacket pocket and produced a brown snakeskin billfold wallet. The hooded man snatched it from Griffin's trembling hand. Lowering the blade from his throat he slashed it across Griffin's stomach and fled. Griffin staggered, clutching his stomach, blood seeping through his white dress shirt. Unaware of what had just happened, Samantha's irritation at being kept waiting turned to shock as she let out a loud, piercing scream as he slumped to the sidewalk next to the open door of the cab.

In an alleyway a quarter of a mile away, Koskov pulled down the hood and examined the wallet. He looked at the assorted high end credit cards then thumbed the dozen or so fifty dollar bills and raised an eyebrow. Ignoring the plastic he took the cash, stuffing it into his jogging pants. He then threw the wallet into a nearby dumpster together with his hooded sweatshirt. He walked casually out of the alley and got into his car ignoring the ambulance speeding past him, its siren shrieking. Koskov smiled to himself and drove away.

The following afternoon Harry Grant smiled infectiously at the Customs Officer at Dulles airport when she asked him to remove his sunglasses. She looked at the photograph on his passport and handed it back to him. "Thank you, Mister Russo. Have a nice day." He winked as he put his sunglasses back on then, collecting his suitcase from the baggage carousel, he strode out of the airport and into a cab.

Arriving at Koskov's Georgetown apartment, Grant knocked on the door and waited. He was alert, watchful, showing no signs of fatigue after his long journey from Thailand. Koskov threw open the door and greeted Grant with a broad grin. He went inside to find a tall, thin, weasely looking man sitting in an armchair by a large picture window and drinking from a crystal tumbler. Grant regarded him suspiciously as the stranger sipped his drink while gazing at the views of the bluffs that overlooked the Potomac. He glanced briefly at Grant with an expression of supercilious indifference. Koskov followed Grant into the room. "Harry, this is Lieberman. He will be carrying out the implantation."

"Is he a doctor?"

"He has the necessary skills required for the job," Koskov replied. "You have brought the device?" Grant placed the large leather suitcase on the table and opened it. Emptying the contents, he lifted a panel in the floor of the case to reveal a concealed lead-lined compartment. He gently lifted out a package three inches by two by one and handed it to Koskov. "It's much smaller than I imagined," Koskov said looking down at the high explosive in his hand.

"It has three times the destructive power of the charge I demonstrated to you in Thailand." Grant smiled. "It'll do the job."

"Is it safe?"

"You could drive a truck over it and it wouldn't go off, not without this little baby." Grant held up the same remote control unit he had used on Ko Similan. Koskov nodded thoughtfully then tossed the device into Lieberman's lap. The thin man's hitherto solemn face suddenly became wildly animated with fear as he gasped and dropped his glass. He stared at the explosive as if it were a poisonous snake, too terrified to touch it. Koskov snatched it up and held it in front of Lieberman's face.

"You need to get a hold of yourself," Koskov said viciously. "You've got a job to do and you'd better do it right, got it?" He jabbed Lieberman in the chest with the device then threw it back to

Grant.

"When do we do it?" Grant asked.

"Tonight." Koskov's voice was cold and steady. "We do it tonight."

Lamp Post Lane was soundless and tranquil at 3am as Grant bypassed the alarm to the Griffin residence. The three men stood together in the hallway, their white flash-light beams piercing the darkness. Koskov led the way up the stairs and into the master bedroom. Griffin and Samantha were sleeping in two large beds separated by a pair of nineteenth century French walnut cabinets. Griffin stirred restlessly. It had been just over twenty-four hours since he had been treated at the Emergency Room for the knife wound to his stomach and, despite the pain relief, it caused him severe discomfort every time he moved.

Lieberman tentatively walked between the beds. Reaching into his medical bag he produced two small, three inch long metal cannisters and handed one to Koskov. Lieberman held the cannister close to Samantha's nose and, holding a mask to his face, began to spray the colourless gas. The Halothane hissed quietly out of the cannister, Samantha inhaling it as she slept. She stirred momentarily then lay quietly, completely anaesthetised. Koskov had already begun to repeat the process on Griffin who, after coughing briefly, was also now sound asleep.

Koskov slapped Griffin's face hard with no response. Lieberman looked at him apprehensively. "Just checking," Koskov said removing his mask. Grant switched on the lights and grabbed Griffin's duvet and pillows, throwing them onto the floor. He then picked up the sleeping man in his powerful arms while Koskov spread a large plastic sheet over the bed. Grant then unceremoniously dropped him on top of it.

Lieberman pulled on a pair of surgical gloves and knelt down beside the bed while Koskov and Grant removed Griffin's silver striped silk pyjamas. Gently Lieberman removed the large dressing to reveal the sutured wound. After sterilising the area he took a pair of small scissors to cut the sutures then hesitated. "Get on with it," Koskov growled. He always knew that using the struck-off surgeon was going to be problematic but the man was proving to be a liability.

After a few minutes Lieberman had removed the stitches. Using a scalpel he made a six inch incision, cutting through into the abdominal cavity. He swabbed furiously as the blood poured from the incision. There's too much blood. I can't see a thing," he whined, desperately trying to see into the man's abdomen. "It's no good, I can't do it under these conditions." He threw the scalpel and swabs down in defeat.

"Let me explain something to you, doctor," Koskov said picking up the scalpel and holding it to Lieberman's face. "You get this done and get paid handsomely for it or," he pressed the tip of the blade so it drew a speck of blood, "I'll have to do it which then makes you, redundant. Understand?"

"Yes," Lieberman stammered, trying not to move his head. "I can do this." Koskov slowly lowered the scalpel and gave it back to him.

"Then get on with it." He slapped it into Lieberman's hand.

Fifteen minutes later and with the incision clamped open,

Lieberman announced that he was ready to implant the device. As Grant handed it to him, Lieberman's hand shook as he took it from him. He swallowed hard and inserted it into the cavity, securing it against the large intestine. Finally, at a little after 4am, he had finished. Having re-sutured the incision he replaced the dressing, packed away his instruments and removed his gloves. Grant and Koskov set to work cleaning up, washing the blood off Griffin's body and then redressing him in his pyjamas. By 4.30am all trace that they had ever been there had been removed.

The three men remained silent as Koskov drove them back towards the city. The implantation of the explosive device had gone according to plan. Griffin's wound would now heal with the bomb inside him. Completely undetectable, Griffin would now be able to successfully pass through the security scans both at the White House and in Iceland. Koskov smiled as he considered the fact that nobody knew that Griffin had become the unwitting instrument of a political assassination.

Lieberman, who had become increasingly edgy since leaving the Griffin house, asked to be let out of the car. Koskov looked at the fidgeting man on the back seat in the mirror. "It's a long walk back into the city."

"I'll get a cab," he said quickly. Koskov agreed and pulled over. Lieberman jumped out and began walking away. Koskov pulled in front of him and stopped, winding down the window.

"Lieberman, haven't you forgotten something?" he called, smiling. Lieberman looked at him nervously. "Your payment," Koskov said. Lieberman relaxed a little as Koskov added, "I've got it right here."

It was 5.45am by the time Grant and Koskov had returned to Koskov's apartment. "When do you plan to leave for Iceland?" Koskov asked, handing Grant a large black coffee. He took it and eased himself back in the armchair by the window.

"In a few days. I thought I might take some time out in New York first. Kick back a little. Grab a chilli-dog or two, take in a Yankees game, walk down Madison Avenue. It's been two years since I've been in the States, I miss the pollution." Grant gazed out of the window as the sun began to rise over the Potomac. Koskov studied him as he drank his coffee. Although he was satisfied with Grant's plan and the execution of it thus far, it concerned him that Grant was keeping much of the detail to himself. He couldn't afford the possibility of anything going wrong. General Durov had made it quite clear what would happen to him if the operation was anything but a complete success.

"How do you plan to get into Iceland? By air?"

"No, too risky, even using a different name. There's a guy I know in Norway has a charter business out of Oslo. He'll fly me out and I'll do a HALO jump into the sea, then a long distance underwater swim from three miles out."

"And your exit plan?"

"You don't need to worry about that, it's taken care of." He allowed a knowing smile to flicker across his face. "Just make sure you let me have the rest of my money."

"And Mabbitt," Koskov added. The smile vanished and was replaced by a tortured combination of grief and hatred.

"Yes, and Mabbitt."

Five miles away, beneath the off-ramp of the Capital Beltway leading to River Road, a DC Metro cop got out of his patrol car. He walked over to a man's body and bent down to examine it. The body lay face-down, his long, thin limbs were twisted and broken. The cop looked up at the Beltway high above him. The position of the body and the injuries sustained certainly pointed to a fall. It was only when he turned the man over and saw his throat had been cut with a single deep slash that he decided to call in homicide. He searched the man's pockets, took out a driver's licence and read the name. "Well, Mister Lieberman," he said comparing the photograph with the dead man. "It looks like somebody out there really didn't like you at all."

General Durov opened the door to his Moscow apartment and told General Guskov to come inside. "We agreed that we should not meet again until after the operation," Durov said angrily. Guskov's face was grave.

"What do you think you are doing, Nikolai, antagonising the Americans this close to the summit?" Guskov said looking flustered and agitated. "Understanding the Americans' cowboy mentality as we do, you must have known that arresting an American journalist in some childish tit-for-tat measure would surely provoke a belligerent response."

"Calm yourself, Yuri. The journalist's arrest is a considered and calculated manoeuvre. The increased diplomatic tension I have created is necessary to the operation."

"And if Gorbachev or the Americans withdraw from the talks, what of the operation then?" Guskov insisted.

"In that unlikely event I will have taken the first step in ensuring that any future relationship will be far from amicable. Your mobile missile brigades will be safe once more, my friend. Be assured, Yuri, I will not allow the Americans to lead our country by the nose like some castrated bull." Durov poured two glasses of vodka and handed one to Guskov. "The operation is proceeding well and on schedule. I am confident that we are about to welcome a new era of strength and military superiority over the West. Have a little faith," he smiled, "we are almost there."

CHAPTER NINETEEN

"You can't really expect me to believe this. Do I look that stupid?" Colonel Mabbitt resisted the temptation to reply to Peterson's question. Following his arrival at police headquarters, Jordan, Prentiss and Grace had been returned to their cells while the chairman of the JIC questioned Mabbitt. Detective Chief Superintendent Sigmusson had listened quietly as Mabbitt explained his assumptions and conclusions regarding the events of the last few weeks.

"And you say it was during your investigation to try and find this man, Grant that you inadvertently discovered a Russian plan to make an assassination attempt at the arms talks?" Sigmusson asked.

"Yes."

"But you have no proof, no solid evidence that this is the case?" Sigmusson continued, seeking clarification as to what Mabbitt was saying.

"No."

"Just as I suspected," Peterson sneered. "This whole story is just some elaborate manoeuvre to justify you and your men's illegal activities. May I remind you that this all began with a completely unsanctioned operation in Paris resulting in three deaths and a strongly worded complaint from the French Government."

"Oh dear, Neil. Did they give you a slap on the wrist and make you say sorry? I wonder what would have happened if my men hadn't acted and simply allowed the car bomb to go off?" Mabbitt replied sardonically. "This assassination plot is real, you pompous fool, and it's going to happen unless somebody does something to stop it!" Mabbitt banged the table with his fist. Sigmusson opened the file in front of him and took out the crumpled fax taken from Prentiss during his arrest.

"This American that came to see you while you were being held prisoner, Kowalski? Is this him?" He pushed it across the table. Mabbitt nodded as, having looked at the photograph, he read the rest of the page.

"This man is a KGB officer, almost certainly from their Illegals Directorate," Mabbitt said holding the page up to Peterson's face and pointing to the photograph. "He is the one orchestrating the operation and he's using Grant to carry it out for him. Through him, we can find Grant and stop him."

"I agree with him, Sir Neil. If we are to prevent this we must act now. I cannot and will not allow the possibility of this man Grant succeeding, not in my country." Peterson scowled at Mabbitt. It stuck in his craw that this insolent officer who seemed to thrive on being insubordinate to those tasked with his oversight, appeared once again to be right.

"Very well, Colonel," Peterson said authoritatively. "But you deal with it. I'm not involving the Americans." Mabbitt knew that Peterson was doing what he did best and covering his own politically sensitive arse. If Peterson informed the US Government officially, he would then be responsible, at least in part, for the outcome. Allowing Mabbitt to conduct an unofficial covert operation to stop Grant and Kowalski afforded him a comfortable degree of deniability and the perfect scapegoat.

"Fine," Mabbitt said simply. Whatever the cunning little weasel's motives were, Mabbitt thought, it suited him to finish this without any interference from the Americans. This way he could fulfil the promise he made to himself and his late wife and kill Harry Grant.

With nothing more to say, Peterson stalked out of the interview room leaving Mabbitt alone with Sigmusson. "He's going to hang you out to dry if you fail, you know that don't you? I've met his type before."

"Then I had better make sure that I don't, hadn't I?" Mabbitt smiled and stroked his moustache with his index finger.

"What can the Iceland Police Force do to help? Unofficially, of course."

"I would be grateful if you would release my people. I'm going to need them."

"Anything else?"

"As you pointed out, we don't have any identification documents. It would be splendid if you could you arrange some passports for us. It seems we're going to be taking a little trip to the United States."

Peterson slumped into his leather chair as Timothy Haines brought in half a dozen files and placed them on the desk. "Did you have a good trip, Sir Neil?" Haines asked with the demeanour of an old family retainer. Peterson rubbed his lips with his finger, looking distant and clearly preoccupied. He looked up at Haines, suddenly aware that he had been spoken to.

"How long have you been in the service, Timothy?"

"More years than I care to recall, Sir." Peterson smiled weakly and, gesturing to a chair in front of the desk, told Haines to sit.

"I was given some very disturbing information yesterday involving a KGB sleeper." Haines swallowed hard and tried to remain calm when every fibre of his being wanted to run from the office.

"A sleeper?" he said finally, suppressing the tremble in his voice. With only a few months before his retirement, he couldn't believe that he had now been discovered after all these years. Peterson nodded.

"And do you know the most galling thing, Timothy?" Haines could feel a single drip of sweat in his hairline. He shook his head. "Colonel Charles Mabbitt has not only identified the sleeper but has also, it appears, to have single-handedly uncovered a KGB assassination operation at the Reykjavik arms summit."

"What?" Haines was confused. He knew nothing of such an operation.

"Oh yes. The whole thing is being run by an American KGB sleeper in Washington. Somebody called Kowalski." Haines was overwhelmed with relief that his secret remained undiscovered. He steadied his breathing and tried to relax a little as Peterson launched into a furious rant about Mabbitt's seemingly charmed existence.

"Does this mean that Mabbitt is no longer being returned to house arrest?" Haines asked when Peterson finally finished.

"It does." He could barely utter the words. "In fact he and his two outlaws are on their way to Washington as we speak to take care of Mister Kowalski and his plans." Peterson leaned back heavily in his chair. "With any luck they'll all get killed in the process."

Haines excused himself and, returning to his own desk, left Peterson in his office. He thought for a moment. If there was a KGB operation in progress, it was vital that he contact his handler without delay if he was to warn him of Mabbitt's intentions. It wasn't out of idealism nor was it loyalty to the Soviet Union that he would report what he knew. Having already had one intimidating visit from the KGB, Haines' sole motive was one of self preservation. He would have to act quickly. Picking up the telephone, he began to dial then thought better of it. It was too risky. He had managed to get away with it twice before but he wasn't prepared to try his luck a third time. Fifteen minutes later, as Big Ben began to chime 11a.m., Haines replaced the receiver in a call box in Whitehall and let out a long, slow breath, satisfied he had pleased his KGB masters.

As the engines of Grace Fisher's private jet powered down it came to a stop at Dulles International airport close to a remote hangar. She had insisted that they use it, maintaining it would be quicker and attract far less attention than using a commercial airline. Deciding that she was right, Mabbitt had agreed. Prentiss however was uneasy and voiced his reservations. His involving Grace had put her in danger; the shooting in the cathedral had proved that. Although he was grateful to her for what she had done for him, Prentiss now felt the heavy burden of responsibility for her safety. He had felt such a burden once before. When, injured and alone, he had turned to a beautiful young Irish nurse for help in Londonderry. The pain and anguish he felt over Orla's death had never left him or diminished with time. Even now, after what seemed like so many years, the guilt he felt for not preventing her death had left him with an aching empty void. He couldn't, wouldn't allow it to happen again. Prentiss had argued vehemently that it was too dangerous for Grace to continue helping them but Mabbitt had made up his mind and his word was final.

"Thank you, my dear, for all you have done for us," Mabbitt said to Grace as they stood next to the plane. She had arranged a car to be waiting for them at the airport and Jordan threw his now rather battered bag onto the back seat.

"It was nice to finally meet you, Colonel. Look after Michael, won't you," Grace said shaking his hand. Mabbitt smiled and said that he would. He got into the brown Chrysler LeBaron next to Jordan, who was looking at the passport he had just shown to the US Customs official.

"Thord Arfsten!" he muttered irritably. "Do I look like a Thord Arfsten?"

"Sigmusson's passports have got us in without any awkward questions," Mabbitt replied. "Let's be thankful for that. Anyway, I think it suits you, Richard."

Prentiss stood in front of Grace not knowing what to say. She looked at his heavily bruised face and gently touched his cheek with her hand. "So, you're off to fight the bad guys again, Michael Prentiss. At least this time you're not alone," she said with a hint of consolation in her voice.

"Where will you go now? Home to Concord?"

"I guess so. It takes a couple of hours to refuel the plane so I think I'll go into DC and catch up on some shopping." She smiled and kissing him lightly on the cheek whispered, "If you ever need a friend."

"Goodbye, Grace and thank you." Prentiss turned and got into the back of the car relieved that she was safe. Now he could concentrate on what was to come.

Personal Retributions

General Durov finished the last mouthful of his lunch, wiping the *Cheboureki* from his lips with his napkin. He noisily washed the minced beef pasty down with a large swallow of *Baltika* beer. As he belched loudly, his secretary knocked and entered his Lubyanka office. "A coded message from London station, Comrade General. Marked urgent." She handed it to him and left without further comment. Durov's face became more and more grim as he read the single page.

"Get me Koskov!" he roared down the intercom to his secretary in the outer office. He read it again, mumbling a string of obscenities to himself as he considered the gravity of the message.

The sound of the phone ringing close to Grant's ear didn't wake him as he snored loudly on the couch in Koskov's apartment. It was a little after 9am. Koskov had suggested that Grant get a few hours sleep at his place having just flown in from Thailand and then spending much of the night at the Griffin residence. Koskov emerged from the bathroom dressed in a towelling robe, his hair still wet from the shower. The ringing stopped as he lifted the receiver. He bristled as he recognised Durov's gruff monotone voice. The General making direct contact with him at home broke every security protocol there was to maintain his cover. They both knew that the US National Security Agency monitored telephone communications to the US from Moscow using the ECHELON system. Furious at such a blatant breach, Koskov didn't speak during the two minute call. He listened impassively as Durov read the message from London. "I'll take care of it," he said finally and hung up.

As Koskov dressed he thought carefully about the situation in which he now found himself. The success of his operation was entirely dependent on maintaining complete and total secrecy. Now the British were aware that an operation existed, the whole thing was in danger of becoming an un-salvageable failure. Such an outcome was unthinkable, unacceptable. Concluding that, other than one man's suspicions, they didn't have enough information to warrant a recommendation to cancel the summit, he focused his attention on a more immediate problem.

Grant woke with a start as Koskov firmly shook his shoulder. "We've got to leave," he said, crossing to the window and looking down into the street.

"Why?" Grant roused himself and looked suspiciously at Koskov.

"It's not safe here now."

"Why not?" Grant remained calm, almost disinterested as he watched Koskov walk to the bedroom and appear moments later with a suitcase.

"I've just got word that I may be under surveillance."

"By who?"

"FBI, CIA, I'm not sure. One of the government agencies. Come on, Harry, let's go." Grant pulled himself off the couch and, picking up his own suitcase, followed Koskov out of the apartment.

The apartment building's underground parking lot was quiet when the elevator doors opened and Koskov and Grant got out. "Where will you go?" Grant asked as they walked to Koskov's car.

"I thought I'd tag along with you to New York. I've got friends there who'll help me disappear for the time being until the job is done." As they got into the car a brown Chrysler LeBaron came down the entrance ramp and drove slowly towards them. Koskov glanced over but ignored the approaching car but Grant tensed as he recognised the driver.

"Richard Jordan," he murmured then looked at the passenger. "And Charles Mabbitt." Grant seethed, turning angrily to Koskov. "Who you're supposed to be holding on ice for me."

"Get down," Koskov ordered. The two men bent forward, the dashboard hiding them as the Chrysler drove past.

"Would you like to explain to me how Mabbitt has found us?"

"I don't know," Koskov said fiercely as he watched the car come to a stop close to the elevator. "Why don't we go and ask him? And then, you can kill him."

CHAPTER TWENTY

"Michael Kowalski, Engineering Consultant," Mabbitt read from the faxed copy sent to MacIntyre by the FBI. "He lives on the third floor, Apartment 301." Prentiss passed Jordan a handgun from the bag. Mabbitt eyed him thoughtfully as he checked it. "Our priority has got to be to find Grant. That means we question Kowalski, not kill him. Is that clear, Richard? I don't want your natural exuberance to get the better of you."

"Understood," Jordan replied wearily. The pain in his back was becoming increasingly troublesome and difficult to ignore. He longed for his farmhouse and the clean unpolluted air of the Brecon Beacons.

"You two go and check the apartment. I'll stay here and keep watch. Away you go." Koskov and Grant watched as Prentiss and Jordan walked to the elevator.

"Perfect, they're leaving him on his own," Koskov said opening the glove box. He took out a snub-nosed revolver and handed it to Grant. The two men got out of the car and started towards the back of the Chrysler. It wasn't until Jordan and Prentiss were in the elevator and Jordan had pressed the button for the third floor that he saw them.

"Grant," Jordan murmured recognising the big American as the doors closed. He jabbed at the button to open them again but the elevator car had already started its ascent. "It's Grant and he's with Kowalski." Jordan banged the door with his fist. Prentiss hit the first floor button. Almost immediately the doors parted.

"I'll take the stairs, you go back down in the lift," Prentiss shouted. Before Jordan could stop him, Prentiss was out into the hallway and through the doors to the stairwell. Jordan swore as the elevator doors closed and he continued up to the third floor.

Grant moved silently, approaching the car from behind so Mabbitt wasn't aware of him until he felt the cold steel barrel of the revolver suddenly pressed to his head through the open window. Menacingly, Grant told him to get out of the car. Mabbitt did so. "Kill him, Harry and let's get out of here," Koskov said impatiently. Mabbitt looked at Koskov.

"What's the matter, Kowalski? Don't you want me telling Harry who you really are?"

"What do you mean?" Grant's brown eyes narrowed.

"Just shoot him, Harry!" Koskov yelled getting increasingly edgy.

"Be quiet!" Grant barked at Koskov. He turned to Mabbitt. "I think you and I need to find somewhere nice and quiet. What I've got planned for you is going to take a while." Without warning he struck Mabbitt on the temple with his gun. Mabbitt crumpled and fell to the ground unconscious. Picking him up, Grant threw him over his shoulder and, casually firing a shot bursting the LeBaron's tyre, carried him back to Koskov's car.

"This is a mistake," Koskov said angrily as Grant slammed down the trunk of the Ford Station Wagon having put Mabbitt inside. Grant's eyes flashed.

"I don't think so."

Seconds later, Prentiss crashed through the stairwell door gun in hand. Breathing hard and clutching his ribs he scanned the empty Chrysler as, almost simultaneously, Jordan burst out of the elevator. Grant fired, the bullet ripping into Jordan's chest, propelling him backwards. Prentiss returned fire but missed as Grant got into the already moving car.

As the screeching tyres echoed in the parking lot, Prentiss ran to where Jordan lay. "How bad is it?" Prentiss said, looking at the bullet wound just below Jordan right collarbone.

"Never mind that, just get after them," Jordan said breathlessly as he fought the pain. "I'm sorry, Michael. It's all up to you now." He pushed Prentiss away and grimaced as he clamped his hand over the wound. Hesitating for a moment, Prentiss looked down at his friend then turned and sprinted towards the exit ramp.

Emerging onto the street and almost unable to breathe with the pain from his ribs, Prentiss could just see the station wagon feeding into the traffic heading west. Stopping a couple of passers-by, he told them to call an ambulance for Jordan then ran into the road. Producing his gun and aiming it at an oncoming motorcycle, Prentiss forced the young man riding it to come to a skidding stop in front of him. "I need a lift." Pleading with him to just take the bike, the rider tried to get off but Prentiss grabbed him by the arm and pushed the gun into his stomach. "No, you drive," Prentiss ordered, climbing on behind him. He hated motorbikes; an opinion reinforced by the number of funerals he had conducted of young men killed while riding them.

With a sharp twist of the throttle, the bike sped off in pursuit of Koskov's station wagon, weaving precariously in and out of the morning traffic. As Koskov turned right at a junction and headed towards the interstate, Prentiss swore angrily as the lights changed to red. The motorcyclist began to slow but Prentiss jabbed the gun in his side and told him to keep going. Changing gear with a flick of his ankle, the young man reluctantly opened the throttle and roared across the junction, swerving frantically to avoid being hit by an articulated truck.

"Michael?" Grace whispered quietly in disbelief from the back seat of a cab stopped at the lights on the far side of the junction. A knot tightened in her stomach. She had never been more frightened than when she thought she was going to be killed in Iceland, but seeing Prentiss again she had an overwhelming feeling that compelled her to help him. She had become involved in something she couldn't walk away from and, in some perverse way, she secretly didn't want to. As the cab driver fumed, vociferously questioning the sanity of the two men on the bike, Grace told him there was an extra hundred in it for him if he put his foot down and followed them.

Koskov drove north through Bethesda and towards Rockville unaware that Prentiss was following behind. Lying in the trunk area of the station wagon next to the two suitcases, Mabbitt opened his eyes and tried to focus. Remaining motionless he listened to Koskov getting increasingly angry at a silent Grant. "You should have just killed him, Harry. You're jeopardising the whole plan by keeping the old man alive."

"He was responsible for Roisin's death. For that I'm going to make sure that he suffers pain of such agonising intensity, he'll eventually beg me to kill him." There was no emotion in Grant's voice as he turned and stared at Koskov. "And nobody's going to stop me. Are they, Mickey?" Koskov didn't reply. As he drove out of the city his mind raced as he tried to think of how to resolve his increasingly desperate situation. Using a madman like Grant for an operation of this importance was always going to be inherently difficult but now he was in serious trouble. Koskov knew that once

Mabbitt told Grant that the man he knew as Mickey Kowalski was in fact a KGB officer, and that he had manipulated him from the beginning, it would be the end of the operation. He had no alternative but to engineer a way of killing Mabbitt before he had a chance to talk.

North of Rockville, Koskov drove into an abandoned cement works and pulled up next to a storage building. "This'll do just fine. You can leave me here," Grant said, satisfied with the remote and isolated location.

"Okay, do what you've gotta do then get to Iceland. With Mabbitt showing up like this, I want you in position as soon as possible."

"No, I'm not going to Iceland. I'm going to do the job here." Grant's tone was matter-of-fact as he continued to look through the windscreen at the disused site. Koskov could barely control his anger.

"That's not the plan, Harry!"

"I'm changing the plan."

"The people I represent insist that Reagan is hit at the summit. That's the deal, you know that."

"I don't see the problem. He'll be just as dead when the bomb goes off at the White House senior staff meeting tomorrow morning as he would be in Iceland. After all, that is what you want isn't it? Reagan dead?" Grant stared his unnerving, penetrating stare into Koskov's eyes. "Gorbachev getting it as well was just a smokescreen to mask the real target, you said so yourself. And I'll make sure that they have no idea who is responsible. Now give me a hand to get Mabbitt inside."

Prentiss got off the bike at the entrance to the cement works and, with an unequivocal warning to keep his mouth shut or else, told the young man he could go. Prentiss stood alone on the side of the empty road. He had watched the station wagon turn off where he now stood and disappear from sight into the maze of towering silos and featureless concrete buildings. He had no idea what was waiting for him. He felt sick. The same sick feeling he had six years earlier as he entered The Anchor pub in Londonderry to kill Donald Boyle.

Cautiously Prentiss made his way onto the site, running between the structures for cover. He stopped suddenly as he saw the station wagon parked two hundred yards ahead and ducked behind a silo. Breathing hard, he watched Grant and Koskov drag Mabbitt from the estate car and into the storage building. Once through the door they dropped the 'unconscious' Mabbitt onto a pile of hessian sacks in one corner of an otherwise empty concrete room. "You hit him pretty hard, Harry. He's still out cold." Koskov looked down at the trickle of blood above Mabbitt's left eyebrow.

"He's okay. Tough old bastard," Grant said disinterestedly. "He even survived one of my more creatively devastating bombs a couple of years ago."

"Have you searched him?" Koskov said. Grant shook his head.

"I'll get my case then you can go," Grant said walking out to the car. Once he was alone, Koskov seized his opportunity knowing that he had only seconds to act. He pulled the stiletto knife he had used earlier that morning to kill Lieberman from his waistband. Gripping it firmly, he approached Mabbitt. A single upward stab to the heart in self defence while searching him would silence the old man for good. He would have to deal with Grant's anger, thought Koskov, but at least his cover would remain intact. He crouched next to Mabbitt, hesitated for a moment then thrust the blade forward. Mabbitt's eyes flashed open. Twisting Koskov's hand, he pushed the knife down and away. With Koskov momentarily thrown off-balance, Mabbitt brought his knee up sharply, connecting heavily with his attacker's ribs and sending Koskov rolling onto the concrete floor. Without giving him time to recover, Mabbitt leapt on Koskov unleashing a right-cross to his jaw. He was stopped from landing a second blow by Grant kicking him hard in his abdomen. Winded, Mabbitt was sent reeling back onto the pile of sacks. "Get out, Mickey!" Grant ordered. Koskov angrily snatched up his knife, wiping the blood from his mouth with the back of his hand. There was nothing more he could do for the moment to stop Mabbitt talking.

"Just remember you've got a job to do, Harry," Koskov warned. "A job for which I'm paying you a great deal of money. Stop getting distracted by this man, kill him quickly and focus on the operation." Koskov reached the door then added acidly, "You'll do it in Iceland, as planned, or my employers will consider you in breach of contract and have no alternative than to terminate your employment, permanently." Grant turned slowly. There was a trace of a smile on his face as he stared coldly at Koskov.

"You wouldn't be threatening me, Mickey, would you?" he said in a slow, playfully sinister voice. "You really don't want to do that."

"Just telling it like it is, Harry. We'll meet in New York before you make the trip to Reykjavik. Lunch at the Waldorf on the 9th, right?" Koskov left. Grant's fixed gaze boring into the back of his head. Grant let out a short and maniacal laugh and shook his head then returned his attention to Mabbitt.

"I see you're awake, Colonel," Grant said smiling. "Good. That means we can begin." He pulled Mabbitt to his feet and punched him under the ribs leaving him once again gasping for breath and dropping to his knees. Grant dragged him upright again. "I'm going to enjoy this."

Prentiss watched as Koskov drove away and decided to make his move. He ran to the entrance of the storage building and listened. Inside he could clearly hear Grant's voice and the unmistakable sound of heavy punches being landed. Taking a deep breath he took out his gun, flicked off the safety and went inside. "That's enough!" Prentiss yelled from the door. Grant spun round letting Mabbitt fall to the ground.

"Michael Prentiss. The last time I saw you, you were in the back of Donnelly's butcher's van on your way to a certain and unpleasant death." Grant said brightly. "Yet here you are, interfering in my affairs again."

"Are you alright, Colonel?"

"I'm fine, my boy. Nothing a cold flannel and a large brandy won't put right," Mabbitt said getting to his feet, his face already badly bruised. Taking his revolver, Mabbitt looked into Grant's eyes. This was the first time he had come face to face with the man who had murdered his wife and very nearly killed him two years earlier. He could feel his finger pressing harder and harder on the trigger as two long years of suppressed rage, hatred and grief began to rise to the surface.

"Go on, Colonel," Grant taunted with a sickly smile. "You know you're just aching to pull that trigger." Mabbitt pulled back the hammer and raised the gun to Grant's forehead. There was no sign of fear, just a cruel mocking expression on Grant's face as he stared into Mabbitt's grey eyes.

"No," Mabbitt said, lowering the gun as the feeling of rage subsided. "You're going to tell me about your plans to detonate a bomb in the White House tomorrow."

Prentiss followed behind as Mabbitt pushed Grant out of the building. They were no sooner outside when the razor sharp blade of a stiletto slashed Mabbitt's forearm forcing him to drop the gun. Prentiss reacted instantly, charging through the door as Grant made a grab for the gun. Prentiss fired. The bullet ricocheted off the revolver sending it spinning along the ground.

"Drop it!" Koskov shouted "Or I'll kill her!" Prentiss turned. The knot in his stomach tightened as he saw Koskov holding Grace by her blonde hair, his knife pressed to her throat.

"I'm sorry, Michael," Grace said tearfully.

"I found her hanging about by the road. She's the one that's been helping your friend here, Harry. Now drop that gun, Mister Prentiss."

"If you do that, Michael, we're all dead," Mabbitt warned clutching his wounded arm, the blood seeping through his fingers. Prentiss considered the possibility of taking a shot as he aimed at Koskov. Deciding that the risk to Grace was too great, he turned the Browning towards Grant.

"Or I could just kill your man couldn't I?" Koskov pressed the knife harder into Grace's throat making her cry out in pain as bright red blood covered the tip of the blade.

"You won't do that. Not with this lovely lady's life at stake," Koskov sneered pulling Grace away from the storage building. "I think it's time to leave, Harry. The car is up on the road. Providing you don't try anything I'll leave the girl there." Prentiss grimaced as he watched helplessly as Grant and Koskov dragged Grace away.

"Until next time!" Grant shouted buoyantly as they disappeared from view. Prentiss swore angrily and lowered his gun. He and Mabbitt gave chase. As they cleared the last of the buildings Prentiss prayed he would see Grace waiting for him. As he did so, the station wagon roared away towards Washington, its spinning wheels leaving a thick cloud of dust in the air. Slowly it cleared and as Prentiss drew closer, he saw Grace lying motionless at the side of the road. He sprinted the last few yards and, dropping to his knees, let out a tortured yell of anguish. He looked down at the single knife wound in her chest as his eyes filled with tears.

"It's not your fault, Michael," Mabbitt said putting his hand on Prentiss' shoulder.

"Of course it is!" Prentiss pushed Mabbitt's hand away, turning on him angrily. "It's all my fault. I was the one that got her involved! Me!" The tears rolled uncontrollably down his cheeks as he ran his fingers frantically through his hair. "I am responsible, just as I was in Londonderry!" Prentiss fell silent as he stared down at the woman to whom he owed so much. "She looked so scared." His voice was faint and barely audible as he stroked her cheek. "Please forgive me," he whispered; then his face hardened. Prentiss stood and faced Mabbitt. "I'm going to find Kowalski."

"I understand your feelings, Michael, but we have to deal with Grant first."

"No! You have to find Grant. After all, that's what all this has been about right from the start isn't it? You're obsession with taking revenge for the murder of your wife. Well, Colonel, you've got your vendetta and now I've got mine." Prentiss spat out the words. His tears were gone, replaced by a burning, all-consuming hatred. "And nobody is going to stand in my way."

CHAPTER TWENTY-ONE

Beneath the Dwight D. Eisenhower Memorial Highway, Koskov's station wagon was parked out of sight, hidden in the shadows of the towering concrete supports. There had been an uneasy, awkward silence between the two men for the duration of the short journey from the abandoned cement works. Grant switched off the engine and turned to face Koskov. "Well, Mickey, we appear to have ourselves a situation here." Koskov didn't reply. "I warned you about Prentiss and Jordan. I told you they were dangerous and a serious threat to this operation. And now, despite my explicit instructions to kill them, not only are they here but they have Mabbitt with them."

"They can't know anything."

"They knew how to find you and, in turn, found me. That's unacceptable. Which makes me wonder what else do they know?"

"Don't concern yourself with them."

"What concerns me, Mickey," Grant said curtly, "what hurts me deeply, is that you have lied to me from the beginning."

"Harry, Harry, you've got it all wrong," Koskov said with his characteristic reassuring wide toothy smile. "Nobody's lied to you. I admit not killing Prentiss and Jordan earlier was a mistake but..."

"No, Mickey, your mistake was underestimating me and taking me for a fool," Grant snapped. "The fact that Mabbitt and his two Rottweilers have shown up at your door means that they know about the Iceland operation. You have been careless and, what's worse, incompetent. It is due to your incompetence that I am forced to bring the operation forward to tomorrow."

"And I've told you that I can't allow that."

"You seem to be labouring under the false assumption that you have any say as to what I'm going to do." Grant's voice was monotone and matter-of-fact. There was silence for a moment as the two men looked intently at each other. "Tell me something, Mickey. Why are you so insistent that it has to be at the summit?"

"That's the way my superiors say it has to be done. While the eyes of the world are watching him make friends with the Soviets. It's as simple as that." Grant nodded slowly as he listened to Koskov's explanation.

"Or alternatively it could be that Reagan isn't the target at all and, in fact, it's been Gorbachev all along? Grant watched carefully as Koskov's eyes narrowed.

"What? You're crazy, Harry." Koskov folded his arms defensively, his hand resting on the handle of the knife under his jacket.

"Really? If I'm right and Gorbachev is the real target," Grant continued, "I wonder who would want him dead?" Koskov's fingers tightened around the stiletto. "Maybe these mysterious superiors of yours we're working for?" Grant raised his eyebrows for a response but Koskov remained silent. "You see, I wasn't sure about you from the beginning, neither was Roisin. She was a clever girl, very intuitive. So I did some checking around and do you know what? You were just a little too good to be true. A freelance engineering consultant, engaged from time to time by the US Government to consult on a number of highly classified projects. Travelled extensively overseas particularly to Scandinavia and Europe, always countries bordering Russia. Always in the right place at the right time, acquainted with just the right people. All just a little too perfect."

Koskov sat impassively and listened as Grant continued.

"In fact, if I didn't know better I'd say you were a Russian spy."

"Why?"

"The way you always say Soviet instead of Russia. Only a Russian does that. And the fact that I was being watched by the KGB. Was that really the best you could send? He wasn't very good. It didn't take much persuasive encouragement before he told me what I wanted to know."

"For what it's worth, that wasn't my idea." Koskov could see there was little point trying to deny it any further.

"It was your reaction when I said I wasn't going to do it in Iceland that clinched it." Slowly Koskov began to draw the knife. "And if you're going to pull that blade, *tovarich*," Grant said unflinchingly, "trust me, it'll be the last thing you ever do." Koskov let it go and slowly rested his hands in his lap.

"What are you going to do now?"

"With you?" Grant replied. "Nothing. You're no threat to me. I shouldn't imagine your Ruski friends will be pinning any medals on your sorry ass when they catch up with you. As for the operation, *my* operation that is, I'll see it through, for Roisin."

"Mabbitt knows what you plan to do. He'll try and stop you if he can."

"I'm relying on it. The Colonel and I have unfinished business."

"My people will come after you, you realise that?" Breathing a silent sigh of relief that Grant wasn't going to kill him.

"I think you need to worry about that more than I do," Grant said taking a last contemptuous look at Koskov before getting out of the car and walking away.

It sickened Prentiss to leave Grace's body just lying by the side of the road but he reluctantly agreed with Mabbitt that they had no choice. If they were going to succeed in finding Grant and Kowalski and prevent a Presidential assassination, they couldn't risk the possibility of a prison cell. As they were both still operating covertly under assumed names and without a shred of solid proof, Mabbitt decided that it was unwise to approach the authorities for help, concluding the Americans were even more intractable than the British.

Having walked the mile and a half into Rockville in silence, Mabbitt and Prentiss took a cab into Washington. As they had no idea where Kowalski and Grant had gone, Mabbitt suggested the best place for them to begin their search was Kowalski's apartment. Having the cab drop them a block away from the Georgetown apartment building, their thoughts turned to Jordan as they waited for the elevator in the underground car park and looked down at the blood stain. "I'm sure Richard will be fine," Mabbitt reassured. "He's rather irrepressible."

They stood outside Apartment 301 and waited until the corridor was empty. Prentiss stepped back and prepared to shoulder charge the door but Mabbitt grabbed his arm, stopping him. "There may be counter-measures in place to prevent intruders," he warned. "More guile and a little less brute force is what is required here, I think." Mabbitt had no sooner taken out his lock pick tools than the door clicked open a couple of inches. Starting at the top corner, Mabbitt ran his fingers expertly down the edge of the door. He stopped suddenly two thirds of the way down as the tip of his little finger touched a fine wire. Gently he slid his index finger and thumb along the wire to a small steel hook attached at its end to a metal ring. He smiled as his fingers followed the outline of a familiar shape. Very, very slowly, Mabbitt lifted the hook out of the ring and pushed the door open. Prentiss followed him inside and looked down at the hand grenade held in place by a plastic cup holder screwed to the wall.

"How did you know?" Prentiss said, taking the grenade from the wall and feeling the weight of it in his hand before carefully replacing it in its holder.

"If you play with the naughty boys for long enough you get to know the way they think," Mabbitt said with a wry smile.

For the next thirty minutes Mabbitt and Prentiss searched Koskov's apartment. As Prentiss moved from room to room it struck him how clinical and sanitised the apartment was. With not a single photograph or personal memento either on display or in any of the drawers or cupboards, there was nothing to indicate who lived there.

Mabbitt had been thorough. He had checked every conceivable hiding place, the lavatory cistern, beneath the furniture, even in the wall air vents, but had found nothing. As he sighed heavily and slumped despondently onto the couch the telephone rang. He raised an eyebrow as Prentiss appeared from the bedroom. Mabbitt lifted the receiver and answered with a curt, "Yes." Prentiss watched as a stern, concentrated expression began to creep across his face.

"Hello, Charles. I had a feeling I'd find you there," Grant said cheerfully as if he was talking to an old friend. Mabbitt gritted his teeth as Grant's sickly condescending voice poured into his ear.

"Where are you?"

"Whoa, not so fast, Colonel. All in good time. We need to talk a little first."

"I'm listening," Mabbitt replied after a long pause.

"Would I be right in thinking that you're still pissed at me over that unfortunate accident with your wife?" Mabbitt didn't reply. He couldn't allow Grant to provoke him if he was to remain focused and objective. "I thought as much," Grant continued. "You're not really the forgive and forget type, are you?"

"What do you want?"

"We both know that you're going to try and stop me tomorrow. So I thought I'd give you a sporting chance, like gentlemen." Grant's voice sounded increasingly excited. "There's a disused movie theatre in Columbia Heights, on the corner of Sixteenth and Monroe. Meet me there tonight, eight o'clock and we'll settle this. Just you and me." Mabbitt told him he'd be there. "And one more thing," Grant added. "If young Prentiss wants to find Kowalski, and I'm sure he does, tell him to check the New York flights. Who knows, he just might get lucky."

Grant hung up the phone in the booth a block from Koskov's apartment building and smiled thoughtfully. It suited him to keep Prentiss occupied while he dealt with Mabbitt. He didn't like the way Prentiss had the annoying little habit of popping up when least expected.

"That was Grant," Mabbitt said in reply to Prentiss' quizzical expression. "He's laid down an irresistible challenge. Something he knows I won't turn down. Very clever."

"What does he want?"

"To use an idiom from the sport of ice hockey, a face-off. Just he and I in some kind of duel although, I suspect, without the medieval code of chivalry."

"And Kowalski?" Mabbitt hesitated as he considered whether he should tell Prentiss where to find him.

"According to Grant, he will be getting a flight to New York," he said at last, deciding that it was better he was out of the way at the airport looking for Kowalski than going up against Grant with him. Prentiss nodded slowly.

"Will you be okay? It's bound to be a trap."

"Don't worry about me, my boy. Grant isn't the only one that knows how to play dirty." Mabbitt got to his feet and held Prentiss' upper arms firmly. "Listen to me, Michael. I know you have an overwhelming desire to kill this man but please, don't let your rage cloud your judgement. Kowalski is a professional. You will need to take great care." Prentiss thought for a moment.

"I suspect we both will."

It was shortly before 6pm when Prentiss got out of the cab and walked through the main doors of Dulles airport. After spending ten minutes strolling casually through the departures hall and searching every shop and rest room, he was satisfied that the man he knew as Kowalski wasn't there. He looked up at the flight information and sighed. The next New York flight was the last one of the day at 10pm. Providing Kowalski hadn't already caught an earlier flight, Prentiss thought, that would have to be the one he'd catch. Pulling up a chair in a small café on the concourse that gave him a clear view of the check-in desk, he ordered a sandwich and a very large black coffee and waited.

Prentiss watched the second hand of the large airport clock march steadily around the face as the time passed agonisingly slowly. Two hours, and three cups of coffee, later he swallowed two more painkillers with the last of his now cold americano. He suddenly began to feel very weary. This was the first time since getting off the plane that morning he hadn't been running on adrenaline and the long period of inactivity was beginning to take its toll. He closed his eyes for a moment, unable to decide what was worse, the gnawing pain from his chest or the relentless pounding in his head.

Prentiss opened his eyes with a jolt and looked around him, then up at the clock, 8.23pm. He swore under his breath as he realised he had been asleep for almost ten minutes. He stood up and looked about him again, scanning the faces of the dozens of people milling around. There was no sign of his target. Then, as Prentiss sat down, he saw him. Still wearing the same clothes as earlier but with the addition of a large suitcase, Koskov strode from the entrance directly to the check-in desk. Prentiss' heart began to beat faster.

As Koskov flirted with the girl behind the desk, Prentiss left the café and moved across the concourse to a bank of phone booths. Lifting the receiver, Prentiss continued to watch as Koskov put his boarding pass into the inside pocket of his jacket and walked towards him. Prentiss reached to the small of his back and took hold of his gun. His plan was simple. March him at gunpoint to a quiet area of the car park and put a bullet in him. No fuss, no theatrics, just a straightforward execution. Prentiss replaced the receiver and prepared to make his move. Koskov was only twenty-five feet from him. As he began to ease his gun from his waistband, from nowhere two stocky, military-looking men in leather jackets appeared either side of Koskov. Whispering something to him, they gripped him firmly by the arms and frog-marched him off to the right towards the rest room.

Without hesitation Prentiss followed, watching the three men disappear into the men's room. He stopped by the door and discreetly screwed the silencer onto his gun. He didn't have time to think, compelled to act, he quietly opened the door. He stood in a small corridor behind a second door. From inside he could clearly hear voices. "You are to return with us to Moscow, Major. General Durov is very displeased with you." Prentiss pushed open the door and levelled his gun at the three men in the empty rest room.

"I'm afraid that won't be possible," Prentiss said calmly. The two Russians looked at Prentiss, then at each other and laughed.

"And why is that my young friend?" the larger of the two asked grinning.

"Because I'm going to kill him." Coldly and without warning Prentiss fired a single shot. The bullet thudded into Koskov's forehead above his left eye sending him reeling backwards. "I assume you two boys are armed?" Prentiss said training his pistol on them.

"Whoever you are you must know that this act will not go unpunished," the second Russian seethed as they both reluctantly took out their handguns and threw them on the floor. "You will be found and made to pay for this." Prentiss felt a wave of nausea come over him. Not because he had killed again, nor that he was frightened. But because he realised for the first time that this would never end. The path that he had started down six years earlier had no way back. He was destined to live the rest of his life in a world of deceit and treachery. He was tainted, dirty and it sickened him to think that this was what he had become.

"There's no way back," he whispered sadly.

Minutes later Prentiss hailed a cab and got in. He opened the window and, feeling the cool wind on his face, closed his eyes. As it drove away the sirens of the oncoming police cars filled the air as they sped to the departure hall men's room and three dead bodies.

CHAPTER TWENTY-TWO

Mabbitt stood across the street, fifty yards from the disused cinema, just before 8pm. Having spent thirty minutes discretely conducting a detailed reconnaissance of both the outside of the building and the surrounding area, he felt he was now as ready as he would ever be. He scanned the front of the five storey building, his sharp grey eyes examining each of the eighteen windows that overlooked the street. One of the double front doors had been forced and was invitingly ajar, the large brass padlock lying damaged on the ground. "Too obvious," Mabbitt thought, much preferring the small fire door he had seen at the rear.

Grant would be watching for him; that was certain. Just waiting to pick him off the moment he stepped inside. Mabbitt needed a diversion. Something large and incendiary. Putting his hands into his trouser pockets he walked over to *'Joe's Used Car Lot'* which was little more than a concrete forecourt with a Portakabin in one corner. Now closed up for the day, it was located on the opposite side of the road to the cinema about twenty-five yards down the street. Working his way to the back of the lot through the ageing cars, most of which had seen better days, Mabbitt turned his attention to a green 1973 Buick Apollo. Glancing around him to make sure the lot was deserted, Mabbitt pulled a handkerchief from his pocket. He unscrewed the fuel cap and fed the length of the handkerchief into the petrol tank until it was damp with gasoline. Leaving just a couple of inches protruding from the pipe, he took out a small gold lighter and, taking a final look around him, set light to the end.

Less than a minute later Mabbitt was standing outside the rear door to the cinema having already picked the lock. He waited for the explosion. The seconds ticked by. Mabbitt took the small Walther automatic from an ankle holster and flicked up the safety. Then the Buick exploded hurling it forwards into the air and landing upside down on the 1977 Dodge Monaco in front of it. As the shouts of disbelief of passers-by were drowned out by the car alarms in the lot, a thick black pall of smoke rose high into the air from the blazing car.

Grant looked impassively out of a first floor window and tightened his grip on the .45 automatic in his hand. On hearing the explosion he had sprinted from his position at the top of the stairs overlooking the front entrance to a small office at the front of the building. "Yes," he said excitedly and ran back to the entrance. The door was still the same fraction ajar it was before. Grant's eyes narrowed. "Where are you?" he whispered to himself, wide-eyed and giddy like a small boy playing hide and seek.

But Mabbitt was already inside, standing motionless on the floor of the cavernous theatre between the front row of the tiered seating and the ripped cinema screen. It took him a moment for his eyes to adjust to the gloomy half-light. Then he was moving. Remaining close to the wall he rapidly made his way up the steps, through the exit door and into a wide corridor. Mabbitt stopped suddenly as Grant appeared a few feet in front of him. "Don't go doing anything hasty there, Colonel," Grant said levelling his gun at Mabbitt's head. If you kill me I won't be able to release one of your little dogs of war, and without me he's as good as dead."

"Michael? What have you done with him?"

"You put that gun down and I'll show you." Mabbitt angrily

clenched his teeth. Grant had successfully out-manoeuvred him leaving him no choice but to comply. He threw the gun down and was led at gunpoint up two flights of stairs. Grant stopped him as Mabbitt reached a door marked 'storeroom' and told him to open it. Mabbitt prepared himself hoping that Prentiss wasn't too badly hurt. He opened the door. "Surprise!" Grant chimed, pushing Mabbitt inside.

"Richard!" Mabbitt exclaimed seeing Jordan sitting uncomfortably on the floor with his back against a rusting radiator, his hands tied behind him.

"Sorry, Colonel. I must be slipping," Jordan said wearily. He was pale and clearly in pain. "He managed to get into the hospital where I was being treated. Told me he'd taken you prisoner. He said he'd kill you if I didn't go with him." Mabbitt looked at him sternly.

"If you were still serving in the unit I'd have you on a charge for such stupidity. However," his face softened, "I appreciate it."

"We only need the kid and the gang's all here," Grant laughed entering the room. "Although I'm guessing he's got his hands full right about now."

"What is that?" Mabbitt looked carefully at a small square package strapped to Jordan's chest.

"Oh that," Grant chuckled. "That's one of the little toys Roisin left for me while she was here a few months back. A small block of C4 wired to a trembler switch. Which is why Richard here is sitting so nice and still." Jordan glared at Grant.

"Let him go, I'll take his place," Mabbitt said, but Grant shook his head.

"No, no, no, Colonel. Richard is going to stay right where he is because you are coming with me. As you're so interested in my plans I thought you'd like to see it through to the end." He took the small remote control detonator from his pocket and showed it to Mabbitt. "Tomorrow morning you are going to arm an explosive device Samuel P Griffin has implanted in his stomach and start a sixty minute countdown."

"What could you possibly have done to make him do that?" Mabbitt said in disbelief. "To become some kind of suicide bomber?" Grant could barely contain his excitement.

"That's the beauty of it. He has absolutely no idea it's there. He's going to attend the senior staff meeting at ten o'clock tomorrow and kill not only the President but everyone in that room."

"And you really expect me to go along with this?"

"Yes, and if you don't misbehave, then I'll come back here and disarm the bomb."

"Just like that?" Mabbitt said doubtfully. "And I'm supposed to trust that you will keep your word?" Grant looked surprised.

"Of course. I've got no beef with Richard. He's just a dumb footsoldier doing as he's told." Jordan swore angrily at Grant who laughed and continued. "And after I've let him go, providing he hasn't sneezed in the meantime and taken out half the building, me and you are going to continue what we started in the cement works." Grant pushed Mabbitt towards the door. Mabbitt turned to Jordan.

"Don't worry, Richard. I'm sure we will prevail." Grant followed Mabbitt out into the corridor and said, grinning, "Don't forget to hold that sneeze. That trembler really is very sensitive."

Prentiss sat alone in a smoke-filled dingy basement bar staring at the beer he had ordered half an hour earlier. He had walked for hours, a disconsolate figure wandering aimlessly through the late-night streets of the US capital. At just before 4am it had begun to rain; a cold, miserable, driving rain that matched his mood. That was when the warm orange glow from the doorway of *Riley's* beckoned him inside.

With the exception of a couple of drunks barely able to perch on their stools without leaning heavily on the bar, the place was empty. "Are you not drinking that?" The question slowly permeated into Prentiss' brain as he reflected on the past few weeks.

"What?" He looked up distantly at the bearded barman.

"Your beer, you've hardly touched it." Prentiss looked intently at the man's round face as it registered that he was speaking with a powerful Irish drawl.

"Belfast?" Prentiss asked. The barman recoiled at both the enquiry and the English accent.

"No, Londonderry. Do you know it?" Prentiss smiled weakly at the question.

"I had a friend, she was from Londonderry."

"I got out four years ago and came over here," he said putting his elbow on the bar. "It was all getting too bloody silly for words. At least here I don't have to worry about being threatened with being bombed every two minutes." He turned to the TV mounted on the wall behind the bar and, seeing the story on the twenty-four hour news channel, turned up the sound. "Mind you, this takes me back so it does." Prentiss watched the report of an arson attack the previous evening at a Columbia Heights car lot with increasing interest. As the newsreader moved on to the next item the barman turned to continue his conversation with Prentiss only to glimpse him running out of the door.

He didn't know what to expect as he sat in the back of the cab as it approached the corner of Sixteenth and Monroe. It had to be Mabbitt, the address was the same as the one Grant had given him on the phone. As he told the cab driver to pull over, Prentiss could feel the nausea rise uncomfortably in his stomach. He angrily chastised himself at his self indulgent wallowing in self pity after killing Kowalski and the other two. He should have gone to assist Mabbitt earlier and it shook him that during the hours that followed he hadn't even considered it.

It was after sunrise as he walked towards the two double doors of the disused cinema building. He looked at the partially open door warily. With the booby trap at Koskov's apartment still fresh in his mind, Prentiss gently passed his hand through the door and felt for wires. Confident there weren't any, he pushed the door open and went inside.

As he stood at the foot of the staircase Prentiss found the still, eerie silence unsettling. There were too many dark corners where danger could lurk unseen in the shadows. He took out his gun and began climbing the stairs, his footsteps echoing in the empty void. Prentiss tensed as he made his way through the building. His skin tingled as, his ears and eyes straining for the slightest sound or movement, he worked his way through the building room by room. Then, as he walked slowly down a third floor corridor, he heard a sound and stopped. Prentiss held his breath and listened. There it was again, a faint but distinct shuffling sound coming from a storeroom a few feet ahead. Holding his gun at arm's length, Prentiss kicked at the door and burst inside.

"Jesus, Michael!" Jordan said angrily "You scared the shit out of me!" Prentiss blew out his cheeks hard with relief, lowered his gun and squatted down in front of his friend. Jordan's face looked pallid and grey with exhaustion. The dark rings under his bloodshot eyes the result of hours of intense concentration to remain still, while fighting the overpowering desire to go to sleep. Prentiss looked at Jordan's swollen, discoloured hands tied to the bottom of the radiator and grimaced.

"Do they hurt?" Jordan shook his head.

"I lost all the feeling in them hours ago. My hands aren't the problem," he looked down to the package on his chest, "this is."

"A bomb?"

"A bomb with a trembler switch."

"What does that mean?"

"It means that if I move it'll go off."

"What can I do?" Prentiss said.

"You can leave me here and bugger off and help Mabbitt," Jordan replied. As Prentiss protested, Jordan told him to shut up and listen proceeding to tell him about Grant's intention to use the unwitting Griffin as a walking time bomb.

"Listen, Richard," Prentiss said reaching into his pocket and producing a small pen knife, "I'm not leaving you. I've lost one friend today, I'm not about to lose another."

"What do you mean?"

"It's Grace." Prentiss found it almost impossible to say the words. It was as if he didn't say it then somehow it wouldn't be true.

"Kowalski killed her." He cut the rope that bound Jordan's hands then turned his attention to the bomb. "Do you know how to disarm this damn thing?"

"It's just a matter of cutting the wire to the trembler without setting it off," Jordan said. "But you're going to have to do it because I can't even hold the knife." Prentiss swore under his breath and told Jordan that he would have to talk him through it.

Following Jordan's instructions, Prentiss gently cut through the thick black polythene that covered the bomb along its top edge then down both sides. Delicately he then peeled it away exposing the device. Identifying the wire leading to the trembler switch, Prentiss eased the blade underneath it, holding the wire in place with the fingertips of his free hand. "Ready?" Prentiss said, beads of sweat forming at his temples. Jordan slowly nodded. Prentiss gritted his teeth and, pulling the blade sharply towards him, he severed the wire.

As Prentiss removed the bomb from Jordan's chest and laid it carefully on the floor, Jordan tried to move his limbs. They had been immobile for so long it took him a few minutes to achieve any kind of movement. "Do you know where Grant has taken the Colonel?" Prentiss asked helping Jordan to his feet.

"No, but if he's going to arm the bomb he's got to get pretty close to Griffin to do so."

"Well, we know that Griffin will be leaving for the White House from his home. If I were Grant, that's where I'd start." Prentiss looked at his watch, 07.45. "We've got to get to Potomac Village. Are you up to it?" Jordan did his best to ignore the searing pain that seemed to be coming from every part of his body and replied determinedly. "Let's go and finish this."

CHAPTER TWENTY-THREE

Samuel Griffin limped into the kitchen with a rather pathetic 'I really don't feel very well' expression that so irritated his wife, Samantha. The 8am news burbled quietly from the TV on the corner of the counter as she finished scrambling a pan full of eggs. Serving them evenly onto two plates she pushed one in front of her husband. Taking her seat across from him at the table she looked at his pale sweating face. "You look awful." It had been just over twenty-four hours since Lieberman had implanted the bomb into his stomach and Griffin had been in constant pain ever since. He pushed away the plate without attempting to eat any of it and held his stomach.

"It hurts more now than when I came back from the hospital," he said weakly. Not a woman to usually tolerate any of her husband's self-indulgent whining, she could see that this time his discomfort was genuine. Telling him to lift his shirt, she peeled back the dressing and examined the wound. Expertly she felt around the stitches with her fingertips. Griffin jolted as she did so, begging her to stop.

"There's no sign of infection and, although the laceration is quite long, it was only a flesh-wound so it shouldn't be as painful as this." She clicked her teeth with her tongue while she thought for a moment. "It's possible you may have some subcutaneous muscle damage, I suppose. I'll give you a morphine shot." She replaced the dressing and went to fetch the medical bag she kept in the study. Griffin's face visibly relaxed as, a couple of minutes later, Samantha removed the syringe from his arm having injected him with a ten milligram solution.

He thanked her as the pain started easing almost immediately. "I can't miss the staff meeting; I'm briefing the President on Reykjavik this morning."

"That'll keep you going for three or four hours." Her voice was professional and businesslike with very little warmth. She looked at her watch and told him he'd better get going in a tone a mother would use to a child late for school. In pain or not, as far as Samantha was concerned, Griffin keeping the President waiting was unthinkable.

The rain fell heavily in big soaking drops from a dark slate-grey sky as Griffin opened the front door thirty minutes later. Pulling up the collar of his raincoat, he hurriedly shuffled to his Mercedes parked on the driveway, regretting leaving his umbrella on the back seat. Across the street in a rather weathered Oldsmobile Cutlass, Mabbitt watched from behind the steering wheel while Grant held him at gunpoint from the back seat. In the hours they had sat outside the Griffins' house on Lamp Post Lane, there had been long periods of silence interspersed with Grant rambling wistfully about his childhood. Through all of this Mabbitt had remained silent. He had little choice than to be patient and wait for an opportunity to present itself. As he had sat in the darkness and the long night had finally given way to the miserable murky gloom of the morning, Mabbitt was more determined than ever before that he would stop the assassination attempt and kill Grant, whatever the cost.

Grant prodded the back of Mabbitt's seat with his gun as Griffin pulled out of his drive and told him to follow. Now it was just a matter of time, Mabbitt thought, and he could finally make his move.

Barely five minutes after Mabbitt had followed Griffin out of Lamp Post Lane, a cab crawled to a stop outside Griffin's house. Having suggested to the driver he might live longer if he'd like to get out of his cab and walk away, Prentiss and Jordan had hijacked the car thirty minutes earlier. With no sign of Mabbitt or Grant, Prentiss got out from behind the wheel, cautiously walked up the drive and hammered on the door while Jordan stood by the car.

"What do *you* want?" Samantha said rudely, recognising the soaked figure standing in front of her. She yelled at him angrily as Prentiss pushed past her and into the hallway, quickly followed by Jordan.

"Where's your husband, Mrs Griffin?" Prentiss said, the raindrops dripping down his bruised face.

"It's Doctor Griffin..." she said beginning to correct him but Jordan cut her short.

"Listen love I don't care if you're the Queen of bloody Sheba, where's your husband?" Taken aback at both Jordan's accent and the ferocity of his manner, she told him that he had left five minutes earlier.

"Why do you want him and who are you people anyway?" Samantha looked at their faces and began to grow concerned.

"Is there a phone in your husband's car?" Prentiss asked, ignoring her questions. She nodded.

"Of course there is. What is all this?"

"And would I be right in thinking that you are a medical doctor?" Samantha replied with a simple yes. Prentiss furrowed his brow as the seed of an idea began to form. "Doctor Griffin, we need your help very badly. Your husband doesn't know it but he has a very powerful explosive device implanted in his stomach. It is designed to explode at this morning's meeting with the President. I think you can help us prevent that from happening." Samantha's face went white.

"Oh my God! The knife wound from the mugging the other night." She put her hand to her mouth as she remembered how she had refused to believe he could be in so much pain from such a superficial wound.

"I need you to call him in his car and get him to stop somewhere so we can get to him."

"Michael, that won't work," Jordan warned. "Grant is bound to be following him and don't forget he's got the boss with him. Griffin can't just pull over to the side of the road." Prentiss grimaced with frustration then thought for a moment and turned to Samantha.

"Is there a petrol, er, I mean a gas station on your husband's journey to The White House?"

"Yes."

"If you tell him to slow down can you get us there before him, using a different route?" Samantha told Prentiss that it was possible. "Will he cope if you tell him the truth?"

"I don't know. Samuel isn't what you would call a strong man."

"We'll have to risk it." He nodded and smiled reassuringly. "Okay, make the call."

Griffin's Mercedes turned off Canal Road NW and instead of taking the Whitehurst freeway as usual, took the smaller roads through Georgetown towards Pennsylvania Avenue. The Oldsmobile did the same and followed Griffin onto the forecourt of a large service station. Ordering Mabbitt to stop near the parking area beneath the station canopy, Grant watched Griffin take his umbrella and go inside the building having filled his car with gas.

Clutching his stomach, Griffin, trembling uncontrollably with fear, walked towards the rest rooms at the rear. He saw Samantha briefly before Prentiss and Jordan suddenly grabbed him by the arms and bundled him into the rest room locking the door behind them. Seeing Prentiss, Griffin started backing away babbling incoherently. Prentiss tried to tell him to calm down and that they were going to help him, but he was now so panic-stricken it was clear he was incapable of behaving rationally. Samantha opened her medical bag and began taking out the things she was going to need. "There's a problem," she said looking anxiously at Prentiss. "I don't have any general anaesthetic." Jordan sighed heavily and, with a hard left uppercut to his jaw, knocked Griffin to the floor rendering him unconscious.

"There you go, problem solved. Can we get on with it now? We don't have much time."

Samantha worked quickly. Taking only a couple of minutes, she located the device in his abdomen and removed it. She cleaned it and gave it to Prentiss. "You'd better get going, Richard. Grant will be getting twitchy," Prentiss said. Jordan winced as he pulled on Griffin's raincoat and turned up the collar. He didn't know what hurt more, the bullet wound in his chest or the relentless pain in his back. The only thing that was keeping him going now was raw determination and pure bloody mindedness. He took the keys to Griffin's Mercedes and unlocked the door. "And Richard," Prentiss called. "Don't forget to pay for the petrol."

Personal Retributions

Grant looked at his watch and tapped its face with his index finger thoughtfully. Griffin had been inside the service station for over five minutes and he was beginning to get impatient. He stared through the window at the driving rain, flicking the safety catch of his gun on and off with his thumb. "What's the matter, Grant? Getting a little nervous things aren't going quite according to plan, are we?" Mabbitt said dryly. Grant looked at the back of Mabbitt's head with contempt.

"It's no use trying to goad me, Charles. By now you are almost certainly the last one alive. Despite his charmed existence, Prentiss is no match for the likes of Kowalski and will be lying somewhere with his throat cut. As for poor Richard," Grant ruminated, "by now he will be in a thousand messy pieces spread over several square blocks of Columbia Heights."

"I wouldn't be too sure of that," Mabbitt replied assuredly.

"It's a pity you all have to die," Grant continued whimsically. "You three never made the mistake of underestimating me like Kowalski and that fool Bannon did. I admire that in an adversary. What most people fail to appreciate is my genius for anticipating every move and counter-move to avoid any possibility of failure."

"The truest characters of ignorance are vanity and pride and arrogance," Mabbitt said quietly.

"What?"

"It's a quotation by the seventeenth century poet, Samuel Butler. You could learn something from it." Grant's angry response was halted as he saw Griffin's familiar raincoat appear from the service station, his umbrella shielding his face from the rain. As Mabbitt and Grant watched the hunched figure walk to his car, Mabbitt's attention was drawn to the man's hand holding his stomach. He watched intently as the index finger started tapping rhythmically. He smiled to himself as he read the Morse code message, D. E. T.

"Let's go." Grant shoved Mabbitt's shoulder as the Mercedes drove out of the gas station and rejoined the increasing DC rush hour traffic. Unnoticed, Prentiss drove the cab from behind the gas station building and followed the Oldsmobile towards Pennsylvania Avenue leaving Samantha to call for an ambulance.

It was 9.05am when Jordan turned off Pennsylvania Avenue onto one of the private access roads to the White House. Out of sight of the main road, he was stopped at the security barrier by the raised hand and uncompromisingly granite stare of a US marine. As Jordan rambled apologetically about taking a wrong turn, Mabbitt had stopped on Pennsylvania Avenue at the entrance to the access road. From the back seat, Grant reached forward and dropped a small remote control unit into Mabbitt's lap.

"It's time, Colonel," Grant whispered in Mabbitt's ear.

"I don't think so." He picked up the unit and offered it to Grant.

"But think about poor Richard. He may still be alive. Sitting there, all alone, relying on you to save him." Mabbitt nodded thoughtfully then, in one swift movement, wound down the window and threw the unit into the traffic. As he watched it shattering under the wheels of a delivery van he raised an eyebrow.

"Jordan knew the risks," Mabbitt said philosophically, "and we both know you were never going to let him go." He turned and stared at Grant. "It appears things aren't going quite according to plan after all, are they?" Grant laughed loudly.

"You don't really think that I would give you the means to

prevent me completing my operation do you?" he said wide-eyed in disbelief taking another remote control unit from his pocket. He pressed the first of two buttons. The small red light began to glow. "This is for Roisin." He pressed the second button. In the dark confines of Prentiss' pocket a tiny red light silently came on. Grant started a sixty minute countdown on his watch then patted Mabbitt on the shoulder. "Let's take a ride in the country. We've still got so much to talk about."

Mabbitt followed Grant's instructions and drove north out of the city. Just before 10am, having passed through Gaithersburg and Germantown, Grant told Mabbitt to turn off the 270 and onto the smaller Old Hundred Road. There was little traffic as they headed towards the Sugar Loaf Mountain Chapel Cemetery. Grant sat in the back seat in thoughtful silence. Then he couldn't contain his curiosity any longer. "If you were so sure I wouldn't go back and release Jordan why did you allow yourself to taken?"

"Isn't it obvious?" Mabbitt said looking over his shoulder while casually reaching up with his left hand and, slipping it through the strap anchored to the top of the door pillar, gripping it tightly. "Because you would have killed us both at the cinema thus denying me the opportunity to do this." He gritted his teeth and stomped on the accelerator pedal simultaneously pulling down hard on the wheel with his right hand. The car careered off the road rolling over and over before finally coming to rest upright, a twisted tangle of metal thirty yards away in a grassy field.

Prentiss increased speed, watching helplessly as the Oldsmobile tumbled uncontrollably just ahead. Abandoning the cab at the side of the road he sprinted to the smoking wreck. He reached the driver's door. Dazed and with his face cut and bleeding from the broken glass, Mabbitt was slumped uncomfortably with his chest under the steering wheel. He looked up at Prentiss, squinting as he tried to focus. "Michael?"

"Are you trapped?" Prentiss said pulling hard at the door. Mabbitt gingerly moved his arms and legs.

"No, I'm okay." The relief was evident in his voice. Much of the roof had been almost completely crushed preventing the door from opening. Clambering over the bonnet Prentiss tried the passenger door. First it too was stuck fast but Mabbitt kicked it from inside and it suddenly flew open. Scrambling out of the wreckage Mabbitt looked back at Grant. He was lying across the back seat, his legs trapped by the front seats and the roof pinning his right arm and shoulder. "Do you have a gun, Michael?" Mabbitt stared coldly at Grant who looked back at him with a supercilious grin.

"Are you going to kill me, Charles? Revenge for me snapping your little wife's neck. She'd still be alive today if she'd stayed in bed, but she just had to come snooping downstairs. Left me with no choice, you see. I had to kill her. In fact you should be thanking me for making it so quick and painless." Mabbitt couldn't speak as the rage welled up inside him. Grant looked at his watch and laughed. "In two minutes the President of the United States will be blown to pieces. Roisin and me will have carried out the finest political assassination of the century. And despite all your pathetic efforts to stop me, you will have to live with the knowledge that there was nothing you could do to prevent it." Prentiss reached into his pocket and looked at the device.

"I wouldn't be too sure of that." He handed it to Mabbitt. "This seems more fitting than a bullet somehow, don't you think?" Mabbitt nodded slowly. "I'll wait for you by the car."

As Prentiss walked away Mabbitt crouched down on his haunches and held up the explosive device. Grant's eyes widened with disbelief as he recognised the small black package, the tiny red light glowing brightly. "No, it can't be. I knew I should have killed that little bastard two years ago when I had the chance." Mabbitt watched silently as Grant struggled unsuccessfully to try and free himself.

"Fiona," Mabbitt said in almost a whisper. "My wife's name was Fiona. She was the kindest, sweetest girl I have ever known. She could light up a room with her smile and make you feel you were the only person in the world when she spoke. She was a rare and beautiful gift." Tears welled in Mabbitt's eyes. "You took that away from me." He tossed the device on the driver's seat and walked away. Grant looked at the digital countdown display on his watch. Thirty seconds, twenty-nine, twenty-eight. Furiously he yelled at Mabbitt to come back, desperately trying to reach through to the device with his free hand.

Mabbitt got into the cab beside Prentiss. As he closed the door the Oldsmobile erupted in an ear-splitting explosion. The two men looked impassively at the burning vehicle. "Let's go home, my boy," Mabbitt said distantly. "I'm feeling very tired."

CHAPTER TWENTY-FOUR

Colonel Mabbitt sat in silence, staring at Sir Neil Peterson's empty leather chair having been shown into his office five minutes earlier by the redoubtable Miss Frobisher. Stating rather sniffily that Sir Neil would join him presently, she turned on her heel and returned to her outer office. It had been almost a week since he, Prentiss and Jordan had flown back and been treated for their injuries at Templar Barracks. After searching for Grant for so long, he thought he would feel differently having finally taken his revenge for the murder of his wife. He had hoped for some kind of resolution, some inner peace at least, but the truth of it was he didn't feel anything at all.

As Big Ben's last chime of ten o'clock faded, the door opened behind him and Peterson strode airily into his office. Mabbitt was fully prepared for whatever punishment the tedious little man was about to bestow having drafted his resignation the previous evening. So it was with more than a little surprise that, as Peterson sat down behind his desk, he was greeted with a warm almost jocular smile. "Charles, my dear fellow," he said with an exuberance Mabbitt found not only annoying but rather unnerving. "How are your injuries? Healing nicely I trust? Would you care for some tea?"

"Neil, are you unwell?" Mabbitt queried, unable to think of any other reason for such a change in the man.

"Never better. In fact I've just come from a meeting with the PM who, I have to say, has something of a soft spot for you, I think. She is absolutely delighted with the outcome of our clandestine operation and has asked me to convey her most profound thanks to you and your team." Mabbitt's eyes narrowed.

Personal Retributions

"*Our* operation?"

"Of course, Charles. The Prime Minister knows that such an operation, covertly carried out without the knowledge or permission of our strongest ally on their soil, would have to be officially approved by me."

"Really," he replied slowly with a resigned tone.

"I must say we have all come out of this whole affair rather well." He leaned forward conspiratorially. "Confidentially I understand that you will be featuring in the New Years Honours List. A 'K', no less." His grin broadened. "She even hinted at a peerage for my humble efforts in this matter."

"Incredible," Mabbitt mumbled disdainfully under his breath and stood to leave, unwilling to endure any more of Peterson's self indulgent crowing. "As a matter of interest, what if we had failed to stop Grant?"

"Charles, let's not dwell on what might have been but rejoice in our success and a job well done."

Mabbitt left the office tired and bemused by his meeting with the JIC Chairman, concluding that, on balance, he preferred terrorists to bureaucrats. At least he knew where he stood with them.

General Durov sat solemnly in his office in KGB Headquarters in Lubyanka. A now empty bottle of vodka had been steadily drained during the three hours since his secretary had finally left for the day at nine o'clock. He had read the report in front of him twice and his mood had grown darker with the turn of every page. Major Mikhail Koskov, the brightest shining star of the Illegals Directorate, had failed him miserably. At least, Durov sneered, shot to death by

Personal Retributions

an unknown assassin in an airport toilet was a suitably ignominious end. This didn't spare him the acute shame and embarrassment he now faced in having to explain his unmitigated failure to Guskov and Vetochkin. Koskov's incompetence had humiliated him and irreversibly weakened his standing amongst his peers.

As the last page pertaining to the Reykjavik operation was angrily swallowed up by the shredder, Durov laid his medals on the desk before him. He held each one briefly in his hand before finally picking up the small gold star that hung from a short red ribbon. The Hero of the Soviet Union was the highest honorary title that could be bestowed for an act of heroism. It had been the proudest moment of his career when Brezhnev had pinned it to his chest eighteen years earlier for his role in the Warsaw Pact invasion of Czechoslovakia. That, he thought, was when the Soviet Union was potent and powerful and the world trembled at its military might. He tossed the medal next to the others. It was now cheapened, tarnished by what he had seen his beloved country become. Opening the top drawer of his desk, Durov took out a Tokarev automatic pistol, its finish worn away with years of service. There was no place for him now in what he saw as the inevitable liberalisation of what was once a great and mighty nation. Outside in the darkness of Dzerzhinsky Square, a single barely audible gunshot went unnoticed.

Richard Jordan thanked the young soldier for the lift as he hauled himself out of the dark green Morris Marina. While it disappeared back down the shale track that led to his farmhouse, Jordan stood for a moment, breathing deeply the unpolluted Welsh air, and smiled. Despite all his injuries both old and new, just being home in the wild tranquillity of the Brecon Beacons made him feel better. He didn't regret the last four weeks, he simply did what needed to be done as he had so many times in his career. However, the face of a young blonde KGB officer on a desolate road in Iceland still haunted him. Jordan took a deep breath and cleared his mind. As the wind swept up the valley he took off the sling that had cradled his arm for the past few days and, putting it in his pocket, climbed over the stone wall and walked towards his sheep.

In Cromer, Michael Prentiss sat alone in his flat. He had been back since mid-afternoon roaming from room to room unable to settle. After all he had been through, it felt almost surreal to return home where everything was exactly as he had left it a month ago. It was almost as if none of it had happened. He found himself in the bathroom, staring at his reflection in the mirror. Although now beginning to fade, the cuts and bruises on his face were still prominent and would take some explaining. As would where he had been all this while. He swore and walked through to the kitchen and opened the fridge door. He recoiled as the stench of rancid milk hit him. He slammed the door angrily and, snatching up his jacket, went out.

Prentiss walked aimlessly for a while eventually ending up on the beach close to the pier. He sat down and idly threw pebbles into the gently ebbing water. It was nine o'clock on a Saturday night. Holidaymakers were enjoying the warm evening and the coloured lanterns on the seafront buildings began to glow brightly in the fading light. "Taking a moment of reflection, Michael?" Prentiss looked up at Mabbitt and smiled wearily. "I just thought I'd pop by, see how you are." Prentiss watched the people walking along the seafront above them.

"They have no idea do they, Colonel? That there's another world out there. One they can't see. One that's dark and dirty and dangerous. One that's no place for the innocent."

"We have a saying in the special forces; 'We sleep safe in our beds because brave men stand ready to visit violence on those that would do us harm.' You, Michael, are one of the bravest of those brave men. I know you are mourning the loss of Grace and that is to be expected..."

"But.." Prentiss interrupted

"But you cannot carry the burden of responsibility for her or Orla's death forever or I promise it will crush you. One day you will have to accept who you really are. Until then you will only continue to torture yourself." Mabbitt looked at him sternly.

"And who am I?" Prentiss said distantly.

"I think you know the answer to that." Mabbitt's face softened. "Michael, the reason I'm here is to thank you for what you have done. I owe you a great debt. I know you don't care for medals and awards, although I suspect you will be receiving one anyway, so I wanted to give you this." He took a large A4 envelope from under his arm and handed it to Prentiss. Standing up to face Mabbitt, he opened the envelope and slid out a photograph. His bottom lip began to tremble uncontrollably as he looked at Orla's face.

"How?"

"I had a couple of my chaps quietly 'borrow' a negative from her parent's house yesterday." Prentiss gazed at her lovely smile as the tears rolled down his cheeks.

"I was frightened I would forget what she looked like. It's been so long."

"Throughout all eternity I will forgive you and you will forgive me," Mabbitt said quietly taking Prentiss' arm.

"William Blake," Prentiss said recognising the line. He looked down at the photograph. "Thank you."

"It's time to forgive yourself, my boy."

Hours later, after Mabbitt had said goodbye and Prentiss was once again left alone, he fell asleep staring at Orla's picture. As the night wore on he was tormented by images of faces from the past. Of Donnelly and Boyle and Grant. The faces of Orla and Grace crying, pleading for him to help them were replaced by him laughing hysterically as he shot Koskov and the two Russians. As the clock on Cromer church chimed three, Prentiss woke screaming breathlessly into the darkness. The nightmares had returned.

Printed in Great Britain
by Amazon

84038822R00132